D0278950

Changelings

Book 2
The Book of Raziel

James A. McVean

MCVEANJIM@ aol.com

Cover art by James Hare
Jameshare @gmail.com

DEDICATIONS

To Nicola and Freya,
and our wee twins xx
*

For Beth, enjoy!
*

For Phil, the Welsh Wizard,
your constant queries about Book2
drove me mad,
cheers mate!
*

For Ann and John.
Your enthusiasm for Book 1
encouraged and delighted me.
Thank you!
*

To Billy Cassidy,
hope this one lasts you longer
than a single train trip!

The Changeling Prophecy

When Netherworld's Children are
Scattered and Scorched.

When a Maiden Wields an Angelic Sword
with a Dragon's bite.

When Shadows Creep
with Evil Intent.

When Bloody Revenge
Rises from the depths.

When Raziel's Legacy is Sought
and Found.

When the Threshold is Crossed
and Conquered.

When Shapeless Ghosts
are Made Solid.

When Frozen Tears
Form a Bridge.

The Changelings will Fly from Darkhaven
and Banish the Darkness.

Chapter1

Rubbing his freezing hands together, the young guard attempted to warm them over the glowing embers of the brazier.

"It helps if you slacken the straps and stick 'em behind your breastplate, son." The older guard offered kindly, his breath crystallising in the cold night air.

"Cheers." He copied his partner, tucking his hands in behind his thick leather armour.

"What about me feet? Mine are like blocks of ice."

The old guard laughed.

"Just stamp them, lad, or march. But don't let Captain Reed spot you away from the post, or he'll be wearing your guts for garters in the morning."

A deep rumble of thunder interrupted their banter. A puzzled look crossed the older guard's face, for it was a cold cloudless night. The young guard peered around nervously into the gloom: the field was empty except for the massive burial mounds in the distance, the blackened earth dusted with a moon reflecting sparkle of frost.

"Don't worry lad, there hasn't been a Demon sighted for over a month now. The Captain says they probably wont come back this way, not with the Changelings here."

"You were there, right? At the battle with the demons. They say that the Goddess herself rose from the earth, right over there." He pointed into the darkness.

The older guard nodded solemnly. "I stood with Lord Ness and the Changelings, when young Jack flew from the sky in his Dragon form," he began, the young guard hanging on his every word. "Yep, that was some night. He swooped down with the Angels just as the Demons began to attack. Then the ground shakes and Danu herself rises from the earth, all rocks and fire! She only takes away the Demon's magic and leaves us to fight them..."

"Tell us about the fire!" The young guard interrupted excitedly.

"Give us peace, you impatient pup," he snapped.

"There was thousands of them, all teeth and claws, bloody deadly things they were. But we fought long and hard, must've killed a couple of dozen of them myself."

The older guard shuddered and pulled his cloak tighter about his shoulders, before continuing in a whisper. "There was just too many of them, too many. I lost loads o' good mates that night, not just soldiers either mind, city folks stood with us too. Good men all."

He sniffed his eyes watering with more than the cold night air.

"But Jack and the Angels did something miraculous that night. Somehow they made a gigantic fireball in the sky, brighter than the midday sun it was, and they just dropped it bang in the middle of the monsters. You should have seen it, the heat was terrible. I lost me damn eyebrows. The surviving Demons turned tail and fled. But Jack and the Angels fell, crashed into the ashes. We thought young Jack was a goner, but he is made of sterner stuff. He was laid up for a few months before him and that warrior girl - Samanthiel - started hunting down the last of the Demons."

"Have you seen his bone armour?" The younger guard cut in again. "They say it's the magical bones of Ulfner Darkbane no less!"

"Yep, he was wearing it once he changed back into a person. They say that it is indeed Ulfner's bones, gotten from deep within a mountain where the Dragons were, way up

North in the Giant's Teeth Mountains. No blade can pierce that armour, wouldn't mind some myself." He ended with a wry grin.

Suddenly a flash of lightning burst through the sky and hit one of the distant burial mounds, and for a brief moment the young guard thought he could see a figure appear silhouetted on the smoking hilltop. Both shielded their eyes, their night vision destroyed by the brightness.

"I think ... I saw something."

The old guard scowled. "Don't be soft, lad. Nothing could have survived a lightning strike." He rubbed his sore eyes.

Moments later a soft breath of wind brushed the older guard's cheek, with it a hint of spice. Instinctively he pushed the younger guard to the side and swept his sword from its scabbard.

"Run boy, raise the alarm!"

The younger guard frowned, frightened and confused by his friends sudden action.

A large hooded figure materialised between the guards, dressed in black clothes and cloak, crouching into an easy fighting stance. The young guard stared hypnotically as a long slender blade appeared in the stranger's hand.

The old guard licked his lips and lunged. The attack was easily parried and side-stepped, the dark figure stepped quickly past the old guard and reversed the blade, thrusting it swiftly and violently upwards behind him into the guard's back, the fight was over in seconds.

The old guard coughed and blood bubbled on his lips as a rasping breath escaped him, his legs giving way. The dark man expertly cleaned his blade on the dying guard's cloak, sheathing it before turning to the lad, who had not run but stood with his own sword drawn, the point wavering as his arm trembled.

"Count yourself lucky boy, I have not been paid to kill children," he spoke in a well refined, deep voice. "Well... maybe one," he chuckled softly.

He lunged into a deep stance and chopped the lad's neck sharply with his open hand, leaving the unconscious boy slumped on the frozen earth. Reaching for a silver eye that hung on a leather thong around his thick neck, he whispered, "Dark" and vanished.

Chapter 2

Jack stood at the window of his small tower room. His breath fogged the pane as he stared out over the warren of narrow streets radiating outwards from Lord Ness's keep. Those same winding streets had been home to him for nearly fifteen years now, and he found it strange living in ordered luxury of castle life.

He longed to be out, 'working' the streets, as he had the previous summer; but things had changed. He had changed. He was no longer 'Jack the Hawk' – a very successful pick-pocket and thief, now he had become 'Jack the hero'; 'Jack the saviour of Ness'; 'Jack the bringer of Angels.'

Now he was 'Jack the Changeling' and he could, when necessary, transform himself into a magnificent green Dragon.

He shuddered; remembering the first time he had changed, in the forested hills north of the city. The pain had left him unconscious, but the months of training he had received from his Grandfather Belthor had helped him; now he could almost place his mind elsewhere and enter a meditative trance, as his bones snapped and reformed.

Belthor had opened his mind further and taught him how to change back into human form, by channelling his inner energy by sheer concentration.

The Might Goddess Danu, had removed the curse of ageing, so that he was now free to change without the dreadful toll. But now he felt trapped, he couldn't even go to the market square, without an annoying entourage of children and well-wishers, and to his constant embarrass-ment, advances from girls.

He had saved the day, when returning from the demonic Netherworld with Ulfner Darkbane and his mighty Angels, at the moment a massive Demon horde was beginning to surround the small army of defenders. Jack could still feel remnants of the Angelic power deep within him; for each Angel had bestowed its power upon him as the battle had begun to seem insurmountable. Together they had destroyed the Demon army, scattering the survivors deep in every direction, but then he had fallen, and fallen hard; destroying his magical bone armour: the people didn't know that part; Ness had said it was better if the people had hope and thought him invincible.

Jack missed his Uncle Lupin, the wolf Changeling that had introduced him to his 'real self' and his Changeling destiny. But Lupin wasn't here, he wasn't stuck in the keep, he was off running with his pack-brothers and sisters, wild and free.

But it was not all doom and gloom for Jack, for he had made a firm friend in the strange, warrior girl Samanthiel; an orphan from Ulfenspan - the river city that was destroyed by the Magic Council to supposedly stop the spread of Demons from the west of the country, over the mile wide river Ulfen.

Jack was the only person she allowed to call her Sam, though she still pretended annoyance at the shortened, pet version of her name. She was a tough girl with a strange savage sense of humour, but Jack liked her. They had fought side by side in the great battle that had left him bed bound for three whole months, visiting him daily taunting him in a friendly way, declaring that all the Demons were going to die of old age before they could get a chance to kill even one together.

Jack had sat entranced as she drilled on the parade ground for hours on end, hacking and swinging at straw Demons in a strange, balletic dance, till various straw limbs and torsos littered the training ground yellow.

Jack longed for the freedom of the next hunt, for he and Sam would leave the city, ranging far and wide, hunting the remaining Demons.

*

A firm rap on the door shook him from his reverie. The door swung open to reveal his grandfather, Belthor. Jack was shocked at how old he looked, haggard and care-worn. Though his long beard was still dark, it was beginning to show more white again.

Belthor chuckled deeply. "I am exhausted, Jack. You have been a hard student these past months."

Jack felt a pang of guilt; Belthor had spent the best part of a month healing his wounds after the battle, and the treatment had taken its toll on the old wizard.

"Do not worry about me, Jack. I am stronger than I look," he said, a mischievous twinkle lighting his eyes.

Jack hugged him and was horrified to feel how bony he felt, the large cloth robes hiding his gaunt frame.

"Are you giving away your rations again, Belthor?" Jack demanded angrily.

Belthor frowned, then changed the subject. "How did your combat training go today?"

Jack rolled his shoulders, his muscles protesting painfully. "Not too bad, but you should have seen Sam. She was amazing."

Belthor smiled, Samanthiel was like a daughter to him, but he was concerned about her all consuming desire for revenge. Her hatred of the Demons drove her to push herself harder in training than any swordsman in Ness. He was glad that she and Jack had become friends for when they were together his open friendliness softened her.

Belthor reached up his baggy sleeve, and with a flourish, pulled out a large silk cloth. He wafted it in the air, before smoothing it out on the bare stone floor.

Jack blinked and shook his head slightly, for the fabulous colours hurt his eyes; an endless knot of gold was overlaid on a multicolour background that swirled and changed like wind-blown clouds on a stormy day. He remembered the cloth from the first time Belthor had approached him in the marketplace. That seemed years ago, not the months it really was.

Belthor motioned for Jack to sit.

For the last few months Jack had undertaken rigorous physical and mental training. His young frame grew muscles and filled out to the fine athletic figure of a young man. He excelled at swordplay and physical training, but struggled with the mental work.

Belthor had seen some considerable improvement in the lad; the transformation from a surly street urchin to the frowning young man that now sat before him. Jack had learned that his Father, Lailoken, was responsible for unleashing the Demon horde on the world, or at least the Master Demon possessing his body was. After that he stuck in and redoubled his efforts in everything he did.

Belthor nodded, and reluctantly Jack lay flat on the cloth. He had tried projection dozens of times and it never worked for him. So with a sigh he closed his eyes and slowed his breathing, inhaling through his nose and exhaling softly through his mouth, concentrating on the flow of air and the feelings of energy circulating through his resting body.

Belthor's deep voice startled him as he drifted on the edge of sleep. "Stay with me, Jack. Remember, body asleep, mind alert."

Jack could feel and hear his heart thudding slowly in his ribs, feeling each whooshing pulse of blood coursing though his veins. Slowly, a warm tingling began to prickle the top of his head. In the dark of his closed eyes, colours began to pulse and swirl all around him.

Jack's breath quickened in excitement and anticipation, as he struggled to remain calm.

"Guide the feeling from your head down to your toes, Jack." Belthor sounded very far away.

Without knowing just how he managed it, Jack moved the tingles down to his toes. Immediately they returned to his head and he was just about to try again when he was delighted to find himself floating free of his physical body.

Jack floated in a sea of pulsating colour and with each beat of his heart a pulse of blue light radiated outwards from his prone body, through a thin line of the brightest white, growing from his physical form and connecting to his spiritual body between his shoulder blades.

Below him, Belthor's aura blazed with golden light, almost unbearably bright.

"Try and move, Jack." Belthor's voice echoed slightly as if here was shouting in a cave.

Jack tried to walk through the air, but felt foolish as his glowing legs swished back and forth in mid-air. Then he remembered that to move anywhere in the astral realms he had to think it, then move.

"Remember your lessons, Jack." Belthor chuckled.

Jack glanced over to the far wall and willed himself over there. Suddenly he shot across the room, coming to an abrupt halt, bobbing like a bizarre balloon.

I wonder what it's like outside, he thought to himself absently.

"Wait... Jack." Belthor cried, too late.

No sooner had he finished the thought, Jack passed swiftly through the wall, as if it were made from smoke, out into the night at high speed.

Jack carried on at a tremendous rate till he shouted 'Stop' in his mind.

Now he floated high above the city, some distance from the keep, the thin cord of light still attaching him to his body. He took stock of his situation and his senses were nearly overwhelmed by the sheer beauty of the Astral realms; every house, every brick in fact, radiated sparkling lights of every colour. Every tree lining the main road to the keep glowed with a fire of the brightest green. Then he noticed the people; each person was enveloped in a glowing sheath of colour, some flared bright, whilst others were more muted.

Casting his eyes skyward, Jack realised that he could see the wind; great swirling purple eddies and currents flowing through the night sky. He hung there awestruck for what seemed like an eternity, before something below tugged at his attention.

A darkness moved through the streets below, creeping slowly and steadily through the city, in the direction of the keep.

His curiosity piqued, Jack made himself float closer to investigate. It was a man-shaped darkness, weaving stealthily between the pedestrians out and about on that evening.

Two patrolling guards turned into the street. Instantly the black shape stopped dead still, then crept into the shadows of a nearby alley. Jack felt a growing sensation of dread swirling where his stomach should have been.

"Guards!" he cried. "Look over there, in the alley!"

The two guards passed right beneath him, chatting away, oblivious to the spirit floating above their heads.

Once again the shape began to move, heading into the street, towards Lord Ness's keep. Jack moved and placed himself between the shape and the keep, but it did not stop. The dark figure passed clean through his spirit, leaving him feeling ill, as a wave of sick dread swept through him; for in that instant he knew what was going to happen.

Chapter 3

The shadow moved swiftly now, speeding towards the steps of the keep and an innocent doorman taking a few puffs of his favourite pipe. Moments later the bright aura of the servant turned deep red, fading slowly before winking out as he fell, lifeless, down the stone steps.

Panic gripped Jack's soul and he cast an anxious glance at his room window high above. He thought himself upwards, but his state of mind sent him shooting far too high, as he rose like a firework into the night.

"Belthor!" he cried desperately. "Someone is coming!"

Jack forced himself to calm down for a moment, before concentrating on returning to his physical body. He barely perceived the dark shadow looming over his body, and with a violent snap Jack was back.

"Shield!" He cried sitting swiftly, diving into a roll. A blade clattered against the shield that had magically appeared on his arm.

"Sword!" he called, rising and circling uncertainly. The shield transformed into a fiery long sword; the fantastic weapon had been gifted to him by Ulfner Darkbane, an ancient hero from times past. He merely needed to say the weapon and it would appear and instantly transform.

Suddenly there was a bright flash followed closely by a metallic tinkle, as something rolled across the floor to stop at Jack's feet. The assassin was invisible no longer, for Samanthiel's slender blade - Nemesis - now rested under the jutting chin that protruded from the cowled hood.

Samanthiel stood there decked in padded training armour, flushed and panting, holding her beautifully engraved weapon at arm's length, as if it weighed no more than a feather.

"You know, it's strange." She began in a light tone laced with deadly menace. "As soon as I touched my sword. I could see this dark creature creeping though the corridor. So I decided to follow it and see just where we ended up going."

Without a word the assassin threw himself backwards over Jack's bed, performing a back flip and landing with a throwing dagger in each gloved hand.

"Stop." Belthor commanded magically, as he appeared in the open doorway.

The man gave a nasty chuckle and swivelled smoothly, hurling a dagger at the old man. It slammed into Belthor's right shoulder, sending him sprawling backwards into the corridor.

Samanthiel's eyes narrowed as the man produced another blade, this one long and slender with a wicked point. He proceeded to whirl the two blades in unison, creating a whistling silver blur. Samanthiel snarled as she and Jack leapt to attack the man who had just injured their friend.

Each thrust and slash was easily parried and counter-ed, and in moments both Jack and Samanthiel were breath-ing heavily, each bleeding from a single small cut on the cheek.

A commotion sounded from the corridor and several armed housemen poured into the room. These guards were renown for their discipline and bravery, having been chosen from among the finest fighters in the land.

Instantly the man lowered his two blades, smoothly sheathing both of them. For a moment or two nobody moved, then the housemen moved slowly forwards, grim determination in their eyes, while Jack cast a glance at Belthor who was slumped on the floor. He was bleeding heavily from his shoulder wound, pale with shock.

"Watch him carefully," Belthor panted. "This is Garan Snare!"

The advancing guards halted, casting nervous glances at each other. Jack turned and stared at the hooded figure in black, every one had heard of the Garan Snare; an infamous assassin from distant Grimswade.

Garan Snare lowered his hood, to reveal a face crisscrossed with old scars. His long black hair was tied in a tail and tucked behind his cloak. Jack noticed that half of the man's right ear was missing, in a bite shaped curl. As he stood staring at the killer, he in turn stared right into Jack's eyes, unflinching like a predator eyeing his prey.

"What brings you to Ness, Snare?" Belthor demanded, hobbling into the room.

Garan Snare didn't acknowledge him, as he continued to stare intently at Jack.

Belthor reddened and stepped closer repeating himself. This time the assassin slowly turned his head and smiled at the old wizard.

"That is a stupid question, old man. You know I am here for the demon boy. Dead or alive, it doesn't matter to me, either way he will be coming with me."

Jack's already racing pulse quickened. *Demon boy?* He thought to himself.

The guards formed a barrier between Snare and the lad, much to Jack's chagrin. Samanthiel moved in closer to his side, raising her small shield; ready to deflect any thrown weapon.

Belthor stepped closer raising his arm, a large drip of dark blood fell from his outstretched finger tip.

"Come any closer and you will lose that arm, mage," Snare hissed.

Belthor wasn't about to, instead he closed his eyes, summoning power from deep within the earth. The room started vibrating slightly with the building energy.

Garan Snare heaved a sigh and closed his left hand around a large ruby that hung on a silver chain around his neck.

"Oh well. You'll do instead." Snare leapt at Belthor and grabbed his bloody hand.

"Home!" He shouted.

Then the room exploded.

Jack and Samanthiel were thrown backwards against the wall as a sphere of lightning shot upwards, bursting through the roof in a shower of broken tiles and timbers.

"Shield." Jack cried through the choking dust and debris. He held the shield above them both as stone and wood exploded harmlessly against its magical surface. As the dust settled the pair slumped to the floor, staring up through the gaping hole in the roof at the small flash of light speeding eastwards through the night sky.

*

The old man sat alone at a large table piled high with scrolls and parchments. His normally well kept appearance now unkempt and haggard. He drew a deep breath and exhaled a heavy sigh, before standing shakily on thin legs.

Trade had recently petered out with the distant city states of Haarsfaldt and Grimswade, and the city's supplies of spices and meats were rapidly dwindling. Food rationing was very unpopular, but very necessary, for the recent demonic battle had left the surrounding farmlands dead and empty.

Lord Ness was beyond tired, everything was literally falling to pieces around him; now half of his home was in ruins and the teacher of the magic school and best friend was missing.

Ness left his study and made his way up a half blocked spiral stairway to the remnants of Jack's room. A dozen servants and guards laboured long hours digging in the rubble, but the frantic search was in vain for he had lost four good housemen in the explosion.

*

Jack lay against the stone wall, fat tears formed in his bloodshot eyes and rolled down his bruised cheeks. He opened and closed his mouth, licking his swollen lips; tasting the metallic tang of blood, trickling in a thin red line from his damaged nose.

Lord Ness knelt in front of him speaking, but the words were muffled and meaningless as the room seemed to buckle and spin beneath him. Jack felt really drowsy and he began to slowly close his eyes. Lord Ness's expression grew grave and he placed long cool fingers either side of Jack's throbbing head. Moments later he was washed with sound as his hearing healed and his spinning head cleared. He opened his eyes to see Lord Ness's back as he knelt between Samanthiel's splayed legs, his fingertips glowing with healing energy.

"Thank the Gods!" Lord Ness exclaimed as Jack began to move. "We didn't think anyone could have survived that explosion."

Two servants lifted Samanthiel, carrying her from the room.

"Sam? Is she...," Jack began to ask tentatively.

"She has been taken for further healing, Jack, but thankfully I feel she will pull through. She is a very tough young lady."

Jack spied a colourful corner amongst the rubble, and he leapt to digging till he managed to pull Belthor's cloth from the wreckage. He studied it carefully and amazingly it was practically unscathed and the colours still flowed magically across its dusty surface.

To Lord Ness's astonishment Jack rushed from the room, past some servants and down the spiral stairs into the wide hall below.

Jack shook the cloth and spread it flat on the polished hard wood floor. As Lord Ness arrived, Jack sat quickly on the cloth and lay flat, closing his eyes.

Jack tried to settle his mind, but the din from the workers was distracting. Lord Ness knew what Jack was attempting and called for silence. As Jack tried again, he quickly slipped into a meditative trance, and after a moment he floated free from his physical body.

Chapter 4

Belthor groaned, opening his eyes as his consciousness slowly returned. Tight chain shackles secured his wrists above his head, as he lay upon a cold stone floor, in absolute darkness.

He closed his eyes and steadied his breathing, feeling for the healing energy deep within the earth. Nothing came to him; something was barring his energy. A hollow feeling filled the pit of his stomach, as his senses were assaulted by a foul odour.

Somewhere in the darkness nearby something gave a deep gurgling laugh, causing Belthor's heart to leapt into his throat.

"Lailoken?" he cried weakly.

Another rolling laugh echoed through the darkness. A waft of rotten stench swished past Belthor's cheek.

Belthor tensed as an icy breath whispered in his ear, "Faaaaather."

A frozen hand squeezed his wounded shoulder.

Belthor moaned in agony before slipping into unconsciousness again.

*

Belthor drifted back into consciousness as nearby voices floated into earshot.

"All is in readiness, Master...The Council has put the wheels in motion." A fawning, high-pitched voice echoed in the distance, followed by a too-deep, guttural voice.

"Send the assassin to Grimswade, you know the prophecy...ophecy...ophecy."

Belthor strained silently in the darkness.

Riznar and the Council! In league with the Demon! Grimswade... Prophecy... Jack! The thoughts flew round his head, and anger boiled in his blood at Riznar the leader of the Council of Magic in Darkhaven. He raged silently in his cell, thinking of the years he had spent searching for his son Lailoken. Now he knew that Riznar must have corrupted and turned his son onto the dark pathway to possession.

Fourteen Years! Belthor cried in his mind. *I wasted fourteen years searching for my Son, and all along they knew where he was!* His anger flooded him with vital energy and strength.

He began to strain against his bonds, adrenaline coursing through his veins, replacing the raw pain of his wound. Slowly the metal rings in the wall began twist and separate, then with a ping, both chains snapped.

Belthor collapsed back onto the stone floor, panting with exertion.

As he lay in the dark, a small point of light appeared nearby. It hovered and bobbed like a small balloon of radiance, its dim glow revealing several other inhabitants, all in various stages of decomposition.

The light moved closer and Belthor knew it was Jack's spirit.

"Jack…" Belthor whispered with a dry, raw throat. "I think this is Darkhaven. The Council…is in league with the Demon possessing your Father…"

Suddenly the key turned in the lock.

"Seek Gaia." Belthor managed, quickly wrapping the loose chain around his fists. "Go, Jack…now!"

The light winked out as the cell door burst open. Even though he couldn't use his magic, Belthor was a formidable fighter; even in his weakened condition. The two cloaked guards expected to find their prisoner chained to the wall; not running at them with metal encased fists flying.

Belthor crashed headlong into both guards, smashing each in the face with chain wrapped forearms. They went down spitting teeth and blood, as he landed atop them, pounding each into unconsciousness in moments.

Belthor struggled to his unsteady feet and found himself in a rough stone corridor, lowly lit by several oily torches set at intervals. Something hung on the back of his cell door; it appeared to be a ball of sorts, fashioned from twists of hair, scraps of skin and shards of bone. Belthor's strength sapped as he tentatively reached out to touch it.

He stripped the cloak from the larger guard and wrapping it around his fist before smashing the evil talisman. A slight feeling returned to his magical senses, then he noticed a similar totem hanging on each of the six doors along the dim corridor; each a horribly different mixture of skin, bone and hair. As he smashed the next abominable symbol, the door swung open, and the flickering, orange torchlight flooded the room.

Belthor checked the guards were still unconscious, then moved cautiously into the cell. Sickness swirled around his stomach and rose in his throat as he recognised several of the bodies chained to the wall; old friends, good men and women.

A pang of guilt swept through him...*If I had been here...*

Then the nearest man moved.

He hung from the walls, a tattered sack of skin and bone. He groaned and lifted his hanging head, his grimy, gaunt face framed by a knotted tangle of thin straggly white hair. Recognition lit the old face, "Belthor..." he gasped. "Belthor is that you, young man?" he barely managed in a hoarse whisper.

"It is, Master Alvor," Belthor crouched beside the man whispering with tears in his eyes.

As a wild young lad, Belthor had felt hemmed in, preferring the open plains and deep woods, to city life. Then he met Alvor; a young wizard, fresh from the magic college. Alvor had tutored him, as a lad; introducing him to the magical path and helping him deal with the Changeling ways, that had turned his life upside down.

"Wait..." Belthor said and sped out of the cell and retrieved a bunch of keys from the prone guards.

He unlocked the old man's manacles, carefully rubbing the feeling back into his raw wrists. Belthor felt a tiny part of his magic return, and he summoned up healing energy to help his friend. In the gloom, a faint outline of sparkles surrounded his hands as he placed them on Alvor's thin chest, flooding him with vital energies.

Alvor gasped as his bloodshot eyes cleared, and strength filled his thin muscles.

"Where are we Master Alvor?" Belthor asked.

Alvor was a tall, painfully thin man, with hawkish looks; beady eyes and a hooked nose. Dressed as he was in tatters, he looked even thinner. He had a long thin face that seemed to be permanently frowning, but Belthor remembered him having a dry sense of humour, but humour nonetheless.

Alvor's frown turned up slightly, "What do you mean, lad? Don't you even know where you are? Oh and call me Alvor, you are a Master now lad."

Belthor sat and told him all about Jack, Garan Snare and his capture, Lailoken, Riznar and the entire scenario. Alvor sat silently, nodding here and there, before beginning his tale.

"A few months ago Riznar and his cronies overthrew the Council. Any that did not swear allegiance were locked in here and left to rot. We did get some scraps from those guards, but one by one the creator claimed us. They have..." he faltered,

"They have begun an Inquisition, swearing everyone in the city to their crusade of hatred. Any who do not follow are dragged away or chained to the city walls, carrion left to the crows. The white walls of Darkhaven, shine no longer..."

He wiped a tear and sniffed noisily.

Belthor rose silently, his face grim, and hugged his old friend.

"Is there no resistance to them? No backlash from the people?"

Alvor heaved a sigh, "I believe that some have managed to flee into the deep forest, east of the Giant's Teeth. But I think that most of the people have been swept up in their evil ways. It is like a plague sweeping the city and surrounding countryside, turning brother against brother."

"It is Riznar who consorts with Demons, Alvor. I now believe that he corrupted my Son, Lailoken, and invited the Master of the Demons to possess his body. For this he will pay... dearly," Belthor ended in a tense whisper.

*

Together the pair of old mages pulled the guards into the cell and chained them up, before smashing the rest of the repulsive black-magic symbols. Gradually the energy cleared in the cells and both gained strength. Alvor returned the gesture and healed Belthor's wound and removed his chains.

Then they knelt in each cell in turn, casting spells of purification and cleansing on the bodies of their perished brethren; each dissolving in a shower of golden sparks, leaving nothing but a fine dust.

The dim corridor widened into a large untidy square room, bunks and boot-lockers lined the walls, a stand of rusting weapons stood at the bottom of a spiral staircase that led upwards into the gloom. A moments searching produced a pair of ill fitting chain hauberks, and a couple of tarnished round helmets with long hinged cheek plates.

Belthor and Alvor helped each other into the unfamiliar armour and began climbing the tight spiral stair. Alvor took the lead, straining under the weight of the armour. Belthor kept close behind, ready to place a supporting hand on his friend's back, his old knees protesting but managing well enough.

The stairs opened into a large, long windowed, oak panelled hallway, lit by dazzling sunlight reflecting through a row of sparkling chandeliers, casting rainbows of brilliant light throughout the huge room. A sumptuous red carpet ran the length of the room, and ended in a grand staircase that rose and split left and right running all the way around the upper floor. A huge double door of engraved iron stood closed on their right, the highly polished surface brilliantly depicted the last battle between men and demons, and the triumph of the wizard hero – Ulfner Darkbane.

Belthor stopped in the middle of a ray of rainbow light. It had been nearly fifteen years since he'd stood in the entrance hall of the Council building, and it still took his breath away.

"Ho! You there!" A stern voice called down from the balcony above. "What are you doing down there?"

Belthor shook himself from his reverie, and quickly glanced up; a masked man looked down on them as he moved around the balcony towards the stairs.

"Follow my lead," Belthor whispered to Alvor, as the masked man swiftly descended the wide stairs. He was dressed in a heavy hooded robe of the purest white wool, with gold-trimmed cuffs, and a plain silver mask with no features, save two oval slots for the eyeholes. He carried a staff tipped with a solid gold eagle emblem, that thunked solidly on the red floor with each angry step.

Belthor stepped forwards with his eyes downcast, and head lowered slightly.

"Sir, the prisoner is dead." He lied about himself, taking a quick glance at the masked face. He could plainly see the widening whites of the eyes behind the mask, and sensed instantly that the man had no trace of magic about him.

He spluttered and gripped his tall staff for support. "Dead? You fools! The Lord Lailoken will flay the skin from your back!"

He raised the rod as a weapon, to strike, but Belthor was quicker, he gripped the staff and twisted it from his weak grasp. Then placed a head butt right in the middle of the mask. His helmet gave a dull clang, and the man's white robe was suddenly streaked with blood dripping from the rounded chin of the mask.

He gave a groan, that turned to a wheezing gasp as Belthor swung the tip of the staff between his legs solidly, and crumpled to the carpet.

Alvor looked at his old friend and smiled a toothless grin.

"Come on, lad. Help me with this damned heavy door!"

Chapter 5

Jack snapped back into his body and sat bolt upright, he felt dizzy, heavy and sick. His head whirled. *Belthor is alive! And in a dungeon!*

"Lord Ness! He's alive!" he cried breathlessly.

Lord Ness stooped by Jack's side, flanked by his immaculate, heavily-armed, housemen.

Jack told Ness how he'd flashed eastwards thinking of his Grandfather and finding his soul in the dark dungeon.

"Riznar...I suspected him, a very sour individual indeed," Ness mused, "...and Gaia...that is a name I have not heard for many a long year. Belthor's Sister, she is rumoured to live as a hermit, in the forests North of Grimswade.

"I must go to her." Jack stood on shaking legs.

"You cannot just up and leave, Jack. There are preparations to be made. If I know Belthor, he will not be languishing in prison for very long." Ness spoke with fire. "Come, I have to help the healers with Samanthiel."

At the mention of his female friend, Jack's heart leapt into his throat; in all the excitement he had forgotten her injury!

Ness, Jack and the guards marched briskly back up the stairs, past his ruined room, towards Lord Ness's own quarters. The corridor ended at a pair of ornately carved oak doors, with large, shining, brass knobs. As they approached the door, the faint hum of chanting filled the air. A pair of the guards reached forwards and pulled open the doors.

A luxurious crimson room greeted them; thick red rugs covered the floor; intricate tapestries of nature vistas in various shades of red, covered two walls, adding warmth to the room; against the back wall a huge four-poster bed was ringed with a semicircle of dark robed, kneeling druids. Nestled among the pristine sheets was the dusty figure of Samanthiel, her battered and bruised body now carefully cleaned and prepared for healing.

Lord Ness strode purposefully towards his bed, a friendly arm around Jack's shoulder, propelling him forwards.

"Come Jack. Join us in the channelling."

Jack knelt between Ness and an old shaven headed druid, squirming slightly, unsure of what was really expected of him. Ness rubbed his hands together vigorously, swept his long grey braids over his shoulders and offered a hand to Jack.

"Just still yourself Jack, then feel deep, through your feet into the mighty earth. Feel Danu's lifeblood flowing, pulsing with her power. Invite it, draw it up through your feet and into your hands and just let it flow."

Lord Ness's words were hypnotic, and as he spoke Jack began to actually feel the surging power of the land, of the Goddess herself. Jack closed his eyes and concentrated as the druids restarted their chant.

Suddenly Jack stiffened and his whole body went rigid as power surged violently up through his body. A collective gasp rang out as a massive flow of energy burst into the room, circulating through the circle of healers. The power of the Goddess Danu filled every fibre of his being, as wave after wave of painful pins-and-needles surged through Jack's feet, through his body and out through his hands.

Tiny specks of light formed in a ring above the bed, then began to rotate, faster and faster, till a shining disc of brilliant light hovered there. Slowly it floated lower till Samanthiel wore a blanket of shimmering energy, that sparkled, covering her head to toe.

She began to move, tensing and relaxing as bones re-knit and mended quickly. As the blanket of light dissolved into her body, she slowly pushed herself onto her elbows, and stared mystified into the ring of faces, then she locked eyes with Jack.

"Oh Jack! Are you hurt?" she gasped.

Jack smiled, still buzzing from the massive burst of healing energy, and shook his head, "Nope, Lord Ness took good care of me."

"Belthor!" she cried.

"He was taken, Sam." Jack paused as emotion swelled in his throat. "The assassin has taken him to Darkhaven, but...he lives. I am going to find his Sister Gaia, far to the west near Grimswade, it was his command."

Samanthiel sat up, and declared simply, "Then I will come with you."

Jack shook his head, "No Sam, I have to fly there. You can't come."

Fire flashed in her eyes and she shot Jack a look that chilled him to the bone. "I am coming with you, Jack. We will sort something out, right now."

"But..." Jack began to protest again.

Ness stood shakily. "Jack, I have channelled healing energy for many, many years, but I have never experienced anything quite like that!"

Jack was confused.

"Usually when you heal, you are normally left drained and exhausted, but I have never felt as good as this for many a year!"

Samanthiel swung her leather clad legs off the soft bed. "Enough!" she shouted, her smooth forehead crinkled as she thought.

"I...think... we need to modify a saddle!" she cried with a triumphant smile.

"A saddle?" Ness and Jack said in unison.

She nodded, as she leapt to her feet, scattering the ring of healers. "Yep, a Dragon sized saddle. We need one, fast!"

Ness's face broke into an easy smile, "Yes, yes of course we do."

He called a houseman, and gave a few whispered orders, before ushering the healers from the room.

"Sit, both, please." Ness motioned to the pair.

Jack and Samanthiel exchanged puzzled glances, before sitting on the edge of the bed.

"Jack, I know you have a hard time dealing with fame and...let me call it...adulation." Ness began. Samanthiel broke into a wide grin.

"But we are in a great deal of trouble here in Ness; rationing is terribly unpopular, and hunger is looming on a very near horizon. As you know, no cattle or supplies have come from Grimswade for the last few months, and the morale of the populous is flagging seriously... So I need to ask a favour..."

Both sat utterly silent, but Jack began to experience a sinking feeling, deep in the pit of his stomach.

"Will you both set off from the main square, under full ceremonial fanfare, and seek the Lord of Grimswade? Try and discover the reason for the lack of trade, and give the people something to hope for in the future."

"But..."Jack began, then fell silent, thinking deeply.

"Yes! We will, and on the way we can kill any Demons we come across!" Samanthiel said, as Jack opened his mouth, about to continue.

She reached over and placed a hand beneath Jack's chin and gently closed his mouth, placing a finger across his lips.

Jack sagged, nodding his agreement. "But I will change here, and land in the square before heading off. Oh and one small detail...How do we get there?"

Chapter 6

A thin wail of desperation cut through the morning mists as a young girl plunged barefoot down the mountain pasture slopes, her long blonde pleats flapping wildly. Her breathing was ragged and desperate as she sped through the knee-high meadow of grasses and tiny blue flowers.

The Demon loped after her, striding easily on four long muscular legs. It could smell her fear and saliva dripped from the rows of its razor teeth.

Her little legs pumped hard as the tree-line approached, she hoped to lose the monster in the forest, but she skidded to a tearful stop as several wolves appeared from between the trees, led by one particularly huge black beast.

The Demon stopped and reared up, on his back legs, to its full height and roared at the wolves. The wolves answered with low growls, ears folded back and muzzles bared.

The girl collapsed in a sobbing heap as her hope and strength fled, but suddenly a strong wind buffeted her to the ground as a dark shadow swept overhead. All eyes turned skywards as a woman dressed in black padded armour, leapt nimbly from the back of the giant green Dragon that now hovered above.

Samanthiel smiled a toothy grin at the Demon, licking her lips slowly as she drew her sword - Nemesis, the blade flashed in the morning sun, reflecting a dazzling rainbow of colour, before glowing with divine energy.

"Gahh..." the Demon spat. "Nemesssisss..."

"You are about to become even more familiar with his kiss, Demon!" Samanthiel hissed as she raised the slender blade above her head and leapt at the monster.

*

From his high vantage Jack spotted a Demon devouring a dead dairy cow, and another smashing furiously at a barricaded farmhouse door. The creature assaulting the building gave up with the door, but the muffled cries of an infant inside drove it to leap upon the thatched roof and begin to tear wildly at the tightly bundled straw.

Rage fuelled Jack's flight as he swept up the valley, roasting the Demon eating the cow with a single fireball.

The creature on the roof stopped and turned just in time to be plucked from the thatch by two powerfully taloned feet and soared high into the blue sky.

Jack tightened his grip and felt a satisfying crunch of bones, before dropping the dead Demon onto the mountainside far below.

*

The Demon's eyes narrowed, then it hissed and began to slowly back up, raising two muscular clawed hands. Samanthiel performed a screeching war-cry, her blade a glowing whirl of silver steel, before delivering a heavy booted kick to the monster's throat. Its teeth snapped shut heavily, and the Demon lashed out with wickedly sharp claws. But Samanthiel was faster. She ducked and lashed out with Nemesis, slashing the descending arm. The blade flared brightly and the charred limb fell, hissing, among the flowers.

The Demon reared up, screaming with monstrous rage and terrible pain. Samanthiel leapt high, did a flip and landed on the beast's back, driving the blade through the back of its neck between its horny shoulder blades, piercing the foul heart, before leaping clear of the dead creature.

Breathing heavily, Samanthiel carefully cleaned the black blood from her sword, the buzz of adrenaline diminished as she wiped the Angel and Dragon engravings with handfuls of grass. Then she gently lifted the young girl into her arms.

"Shh little one, it's over."

"Wolves!" she cried hysterically, burying her small red face in Samanthiel's padded leather armour, as the large black wolf padded closer.

"Lupin!" Samanthiel cried with genuine pleasure.

The wolf was Jack's Uncle Lupin, a fellow Changeling of the Wolf variety. He and his pack brothers and sisters had hunted Demons for months, tracking them easily.

"Samanthiel," Lupin's deep voice echoed telepathically in her head. "What are you two doing way out here on the borders?"

Samanthiel turned so the girl could see the wolf sitting as nicely as any pet dog. "Look he won't hurt us..."

"I think you better speak to Jack about this Lupin, we are on an urgent quest."

"LUPIN!" Jack's voice boomed telepathically.

Lupin whined and growled. "Speak Jack! Don't shout."

Jack swooped from the sky and landed next to the party. He flexed his long neck and shook the stiffness from his tired wings and shoulders, sending his spine spikes clacking noisily, setting the little girl screaming yet again.

"I'll take her up the hill to her home. There might be someone in the building," Samanthiel said, turning leaving Jack to tell Lupin of their troubles.

"Mam, Sander and wee Jamie are there," she sobbed.

Samanthiel lowered the girl to the grass. "Can you walk with me...? What's your name?"

"Freja," she answered, shivering in the cold morning air.

"Come on then, Freja, your Mammy will be delighted to see you safe and well."

She took the young girl by the hand and led her away from the horrific scene.

Samanthiel was surprised by the strength in her young fingers as she gripped her hand even tighter as they trudged up the hill, past the smouldering Demon. "Where's your Daddy, Freja?" She asked with a sinking feeling in the pit of her stomach.

"He's up on the high pasture, gathering the herd before winter closes in. He said there was somethin on the wind, coz we aint seen any traders for months now..." She glanced over her shoulder at the smouldering carcass. "He was right."

Samanthiel led the little girl to the scored wooden door.

"Mam! Open the door! There's a Dragon out here, and a warrior girl, and...and... a pack of friendly wolves!" Freja cried breathlessly.

There was a cry and then a rasping sound of something heavy being pulled away from the door and three sharp prongs of a pitchfork appeared through the slowly opening doorway. The door frame was filled by a large red-headed woman, dressed in a plain cotton dress and woollen shawl, the stout handled fork held in huge meaty fists.

Freja ran forward and hugged her mother's large waist, who dropped the makeshift weapon and burst into tears. A lump formed in Samanthiel's throat as the big woman rushed outside and hugged her painfully, even through her hard lacquered leather armour.

"Oh... Thank you! Thank you! Thank you!" She cried repeatedly, almost lifting the girl from the ground.

Samanthiel wheezed and graciously accepted the thanks.

Suddenly the morning breeze carried a strange sound; a low rumble pierced now and then by a high pitched whistle.

Freja's mother gave a sharp gasp and cried out, "Sander! Get out here! Your Father is coming with the herd."

Samanthiel looked carefully and sure enough, high on the mountainside a large herd of sheep and cattle was heading down their way, shepherded by a rider, and his two large dogs.

She nodded silently to herself, as flashes of light lit from the edge of the tree-line below; the huge pack of wolves melted into the forest and two bare-chested figures began walking up the hill towards the house.

Chapter 7

Belthor and Alvor pulled open the heavy door, leaving the crumpled figure gasping and gurgling on the carpet. They hurried down a flight of wide marble steps, leading down to a deserted plaza, lined on three sides by massive statues of long dead heroes.

A cold wind whistled between the silent figures, the ashes of burnt books whirled and twisted among the legs of statues. Usually the square would be thronging with students and academics, but now the dark windows and barricaded doors stared upon emptiness.

A deep feeling of dread swept though Belthor, he could feel the evil that had been committed here, on the very steps of the Council building. He could feel the fear and terror of the victims, their shades drifting among the ashes, tormented and lost. Belthor moved among the ash, spotting half burned books, mingled with bones and personal items.

"I feel them too, lad," Alvor said quietly.

"We have to help them Alvor." Belthor whispered. "I swear that I will return here and cleanse this place as soon as time permits."

"Time is of the essence Belthor. Come we must get away from here. They will soon discover we are gone."

From the high plaza the view of the city was breathtaking; spreading for miles in all directions, towering edifices, hanging gardens, and the four great statues guarding the cardinal gates. Polished limestone faced every building, so that the city fairly glowed in the sunlight.

But as the pair began down the next flight from the plaza to the main avenues below, they could see various thin trails of smoke rising from numerous fires burning though out the city.

Alvor pulled up to a stop, with a sharp intake of breath, for the wide, tree lined avenue opening below was filled with lines of people chained together. Men, women and sobbing children shuffled in long lines, all heading for the western cardinal gate, spurred along by numerous red cloaked figures, wearing silver facemasks and wielding whips and spears.

Belthor stopped by his old Master's side, trembling as he drank in the details of the horrific scene. The terrible thing was that no one seemed to be protesting, each silently following the fate that someone had chosen for them.

"Move! You unclean Demon worshipers!" A distant voice roared.

Belthor clenched his fists, feeling the power of the Goddess boiling up through the earth, filling him with a righteous rage. Suddenly he strode down the last few steps and across the grass to a slender tree, pressing his large hand against the silvery bark. The tree vibrated slightly and a few leaves and small red berries fell. Slowly something long slender moved within the centre of the tree, rising through the bark, until he was presented with a living staff of solid rowan heartwood.

Alvor nodded his approval.

Together they paced quickly between the columns of prisoners, trying hard to suppress his desire to strike down the guards whipping the people along. The procession of humanity snaked through the city, moving down the wide, opulent boulevards and avenues, fed by dozens of side roads till it seemed that every living soul in Darkhaven was manacled and miserable.

Belthor and Alvor marched purposefully and went unchallenged, ahead loomed the city walls, high and thick, topped with towers and crenellations, casting a deep shadow in the approaching noon sunlight. The massive wall was interrupted by a massive statue, straddling the Cardinal gate. A huge bronze Angel stood staring due west, as its counterpart did at the east, south and northern gates.

The pair of old wizards drew up short of the huge iron bound, wooden gates, where a pair of guards sat at a checkpoint, and logged the name of every single prisoner leaving the city.

Alvor pulled at Belthor's tunic motioning him into a narrow alleyway between two towering stone buildings. As a pair of red cloaked guards passed the alley, Belthor shouted to them.

"Hey You there! Come quickly, I've found some Demon worshippers!"

As the guards rounded the corner, Alvor gave the pair's heads a swift welcome with the wooden staff, and moments later two new guards rejoined the dreadful procession.

"Damn, but this mask chafes!" complained Alvor.

"Bear it quietly, Master. Hopefully we can slip away once we get out of the city."

They passed swiftly between the Angel's legs and out onto a paved road leading arrow-straight westwards across the virtually flat, patchwork landscape of crops and fields.

A line of guards spread across the road, separating out the very young and the old, sending them north along the city ring road. Here the noise became deafening; parents cried out for their children, and they in turn screamed their confusion and fear.

Belthor stopped and watched through narrowing eyes at the thin line of old and young being lead away. A deep uneasiness filled his soul, and he decided that he had to follow them. Alvor gave another silent nod of approval, and the pair split from the main column, heading north.

Bodies hung from the high, white walls, spaced out at regular intervals, the poor victims were manacled and dropped over the side and left to dangle. Their end was slow, dislocated and choking, and their ripening bodies attracted hundreds of carrion crows, and clouds of flies.

Belthor picked up the pace, passing the weary, terrified prisoners, distancing himself from the terrible stench. Alvor had to scurry to keep up with the younger wizard, muttering below his breath, with each mile that passed.

Soon they were clear of the city walls and making their way across grassy plains, toward the darkening line of the distant forests.

The afternoon turned cold, and dark clouds gathered, blown south from the Giant's Teeth mountains. A freezing rain began to drizzle, soaking everyone to the skin.

"What I wouldn't give for a dry pair of breeks, and a pint of warm ale!" Alvor muttered for the tenth time that hour.

In the distance, on the edge of the forest, a dark mound of fresh earth grew, crawling with children, armed with over-sized picks and shovels, overlooked by dozens of the red guards.

Bile rose in Belthor's throat as he approached the huge shallow hole being dug by the prisoners. Three guards stood laughing mercilessly at an old man who had crumpled under the weight of a full wheelbarrow, one placed a savage kick into his ribs.

"Enough!" Belthor spat, tearing the uncomfortable silver mask from his face. His blood boiled as he saw the, soon to be, mass grave. As the kicker turned, he received the end of the rowan staff, thrust into the pit of his stomach.

Belthor roared with a mad rage that threatened to consume him, as he whirled the staff round and smashed the legs of the other two guards. They dropped like stones as the furious old man went berserk.

Dozens of guards witnessing the onslaught, reached for whips and weapons and ran to help their comrades.

*

Alvor pulled his own mask and spat on his hands with great relish.

"You turn your weapons on the old, and helpless CHILDREN! Now turn them on me and face the wrath of the Great Goddess Danu!" he cried passionately.

All digging stopped and the old and young alike stood agape, tools downed, as the pair of old wizards set about dealing with the guards.

Alvor closed his eyes and summoned up power, raising his crooked hands high, till they glowed with balls of purest energy. With a tremendous push of willpower, he threw them at the rapidly approaching unit of guards. The ground erupted upwards in a violent explosion of earth and rocks, scattering red robed figures high into the air. Most landed heavily in the deep sucking mud, and several of the old prisoners, shaken from their doleful silence, began attacking with shovels and picks.

*

Belthor tossed the staff to Alvor and ripped his red cloak off, and cast his gaze skywards, crying to the clouds.

"I bear the Sorrow, I bear the Pain, let me become a Bear again!"

His words became a violent roar and the children scattered as he hunched over screaming and jerking, sprouting thick hair all over, till a massive brown bear rose on his hind legs, easily twice the height of a man.

Four guards ran at him with levelled spears, and Belthor roared his acceptance of their challenge. One guard's spear thrust high at his mouth, and Belthor snapped his jaws on the tip and twisted his muscular neck, tearing the weapon from his hands. Another pierced his flank, above his left hind leg, the pain a mere nuisance, enraging him further. He swatted one man with his huge clawed paw, sending him flying into the pit, a ragged series of torn lines across his chest.

Another dozen guards arrived, encircling him, so he charged forwards, scattering a few, crushing two into the soft mound of black earth, the cracking bones clearly audible over the clamour of the fight.

Then the din died down as more than a dozen black bears burst from the dark forest. Tearing across the grass, roaring terribly, jaws wide and teeth dripping saliva.

*

Alvor laughed uproariously as the guards were overwhelmed, pinned and terrified. He swept one hysterical little girl into the crook of his arm, calming her with kind words.

*

Belthor placed his paws on the chest of a fallen guard and roared in his face. The guard nearly fainted in terror. A deep snuffling growl sounded at his side. The black bear sniffed and moaned slightly at the blood seeping from Belthor's hind leg.

"The pain is slight little brother," Belthor said simply with a low rumbling growl.

"We have watched the humans. They hurt each other. We saw you, brother. They hurt you, brother. We came. We stopped them."

They spoke in snuffles, moans and growls, clearly understood.

"The old humans and young humans, thank you, brothers. I thank you brothers. May the Goddess keep your dens safe, and your food plentiful. May your young grow strong and proud, and roar their songs of praise to the Goddess."

The bears roared joyously at the simple blessing, further terrifying their captives.

Chapter 8

Jack, Samanthiel, Lupin and the crofting family sat around a plain wooden table, sharing a simple meal. Freja sat on a cushion, eating a hunk of cheese. Her father was a large, red haired man, with a round, friendly face.

"Let me get this right." He spoke with a soft voice. "You want me to gather my herd, then get all the other families in the valley to do the same." Jack and Samanthiel nodded in unison as he continued. "Then you want us to drive them all the way to Ness?"

Jack nodded again. "Yes sir, I really do. You see the people of Ness are in desperate need of food. You know the trade from Grimswade has stopped, and I think it might be safer if you moved to the city for the winter, what with these Demons stalking your lands."

At the mention of Demons, young Freja whimpered and cried, "Daddy, we have to go!"

"I aint fraid of no Demon," Freja's older brother Sander spoke up, he was a strapping lad, his father's spit.

"Good for you." Samanthiel flashed the youth a sweet, patronising smile.

The farmer looked at his wife and children in turn, making up his mind.

"It is a long and dangerous journey, and there has been sightings of huge wolf packs recently..."

"Sir, the wolves will not trouble you or your herd, this I know." Lupin smiled, his dark eyes glittering in the fire light.

He was a fine looking young man, with a broad frame but with the grace and poise of a fine athlete, his long dark locks hanging over his white shirt collar and framing a face that set Samanthiel's heart racing.

"In fact we will make sure that you reach Ness unmolested, by anything."

Jack sat waiting, looking at his Uncle. When they had first met, many months before, Jack had assumed he was a thief, but he had introduced him to his Changeling destiny, and set him off on the road to the most amazing adventure.

The farmer took a deep breath, and stood, stretching till his fingers touched the roof beams, where bunches of dried herbs and garlic bulbs hung, filling the room with a sweet, heady aroma.

He nodded slowly. "Yes, I will take my cattle and sheep to Ness, and I am sure that we can get the rest of the valley to follow us, you are very persuasive."

Jack smiled, and rose offering his hand, which the farmer enclosed in his own shovel-like hand, shaking firmly. Samanthiel and Lupin also rose and voiced their thanks.

"Oh," exclaimed Jack. "How far is it to Grimswade?"

"Bout a six day ride on a good horse, over the high pass, and on through the mountains. Due west as the crow ...err Dragon flies."

Jack picked up the saddle and hoisted it over his shoulder, gripping his Uncle Lupin in a half hug. "Take care Lupin, try not to worry overly much about Belthor, Danu will watch over him."

Lupin nodded, returning the hug. "My Father has been in worse scrapes in his day."

Then turned and hugged Samanthiel, their eyes met and he gave her a roguish smile. "Take care of my young nephew, Sam."

"You know I will." She said, blushing slightly.

*

Jack soared high over the moonlit mountainside, finding the freshening winds invigorating. Samanthiel on the other hand, sat on her saddle, high on Jack's scaly shoulders just above his wing joints, shivering in the cold, despite of the thick woollen cloak gifted to her by the farmer's wife.

They swept over a high pass, out over a deep valley of winding gorges cut with rivers, and filled with thick fir trees. Then banking high again to rise swiftly over the next mountain, the land dropping into another dark valley of shadowy trees.

"Jack! We must land soon, I'm going to freeze." Samanthiel called, her breath stolen by the cold wind.

Jack heard her well enough, and answered in her mind, "Sorry Sam, but we must press on to Grimswade, we will be there in a few hours."

"A few hours is it!" She slammed her heels into the soft scales at the side of Jack's thick neck, causing him to flap and veer in surprise. "Land Jack!" she demanded, then added, "Please..."

Jack rose over the next peak, and swooped low over the treetops, till he found a clearing, and came to a fluttering hover and a gentle landing amid the gloomy trees.

Sam climbed stiffly from the saddle, rubbing her sore bottom, stretching and twisting to get feeling back into her frozen muscles.

Jack blew a small flame at some deadwood and got a roaring fire going in moments.

"Better?" he asked.

"Mmm," nodded Samanthiel warming the backs of her legs at the fire.

She reached into the saddle bags and pulled out a water bottle and a cloth wrapped cheese. As she sat and began to eat, Jack took a deep, snuffling, impatient breath.

"Don't start." Samanthiel warned, breaking into a friendly laugh.

A deep rumbling sounded in his chest as Jack began to laugh. "You didn't need to kick me!"

"Aww, poor little Dragon...Did it hurt?" She teased.

Jack snapped noisily with his teeth, close to where she sat, making her leap in fright.

"No it didn't..." Jack began.

Suddenly a huge man burst into the clearing, staggering to an incredulous halt, wild eyed and panting heavily, through his thick moustache and long pleated beard. He was heavily armoured with thick overlapping scalemail, that jangled noisily as he moved, and wore a horned helmet, with a long nose guard, his thick blonde hair cascaded over his thick bearskin cloak. He carried a massive double headed stone axe, the head over his shoulder, the long handle ending in a wicked looking spike.

Samanthiel leapt to her feet, drawing upon Nemesis, as the man drew his own weapon before spinning round to face the opposite way...

"Come on then!" the stranger roared into the trees.

Jack reared up, ready to react.

Samanthiel crouched into a fighting stance, puzzled by the bizarre scene. Then an arrow buzzed through the air, ricocheting off Jack's thick chest scales. Samanthiel dived and rolled, as several dark figures leapt into the clearing. The man went crazy, screaming a blood curdling war cry, swinging his axe in a deadly whirl.

One attacker went down, headless. Samanthiel danced into the midst of them, slashing left and stabbing right, before leaping in an acrobatic flip, and landing on Jack's shoulders.

Jack loosed a fireball, igniting two attackers, turning them into staggering infernos. Seconds later the remaining attacker fled into the night, as the stranger collapsed in a dead faint.

Samanthiel leapt from Jack's back and ran to the fallen man's side. He was wounded, a broken arrow stump showed from his right side, and an ugly gash ran the length of his bare right thigh.

"Change, Jack," Samanthiel cried. "This man is dying!"

Jack took a deep breath, as Belthor had taught him to, and exhaled slowly, drawing power into himself from the ground and the air. He could feel the energy circulating around his dragon body, and tried to imagine what it felt like to do the same as a boy. Then in a single push of willpower, he channelled all the energy into a single word, "CHANGE."

A flash of light lit the clearing, brighter than day, for a few moments till a now naked Jack crouched where his Dragon form had stood. He stepped quickly out of the loops of fallen saddle and bags, reaching in for his clothing, and dressing swiftly.

Samanthiel pulled the huge stone axe out of the way, it was so heavy that she strained to lift the head. She gently pulled the heavy horned helmet from the stranger's head. The face that greeted her was ugly; a twisted nose, and crooked teeth on a face covered with healed scar tissue.

His eyes fluttered open.

"Are you Valkyrie?" he whispered hoarsely, in a thick accent. "Did you choose me this day to die?"

Samanthiel smiled, knowing that the Grimswadians believed that magical warrior maidens, from their God - Elgor, would choose who would join him in their version of the afterlife; feasting and fighting for all eternity in a mighty hall of heroes.

"You are not dead, stranger," she said.

He seemed to slump slightly, a shadow of disappointment crossing his haggard face. Jack knelt by the man, barefoot, wearing nothing but a hastily donned pair of leather breeks.

"Rest and I will try and heal your wounds." Jack said warily, unsure if he could do it alone.

The man gave a low throaty laugh that caused him to cough violently, and blood to bubble at his chest wound.

"I am bound for the Halls of Heroes, Changeling."

Samanthiel looked deep into Jack's eyes, silently asking if he could really help. Jack merely closed his eyes and began rubbing his hands together, while Samanthiel sat watching him, transfixed.

A moment later a faint glow began to form around his fingertips, that grew brighter, till two bright balls of light floated, one above each outstretched palm.

Jack opened his eyes, the pupils replaced by orbs of shining silver. Samanthiel felt the small hairs rise on her arms, and on the back of her neck as a wave of goosepimples swept over her. She held her breath and her heart raced as Jack lowered his hands to the stranger's chest.

The wound bubbled and hissed, as the arrow head slowly ejected itself from between the scalemail links. The wound on his leg similarly healed until nothing but a thick white scar remained.

Samanthiel breathed again exhaling noisily, as Jack slumped forward, covered in a sheen of sweat, trembling in the cold night air.

Chapter 9

Belthor stood tall, a man once more, and paced purposefully towards the dozens of chained guards. Their hatred was palpable, their faces masks of sullen contempt, but he could feel raw fear as he approached, their true emotions showing clearly to him.

A leader rose from among their squatting ranks, tall and slim and clean-shaven, with short cut grey hair; a noble looking man with a square jaw and defiant fire in his eyes. He raised a slender hand, immaculately manicured.

"Stop," he spoke with an air of authority, and to his surprise Belthor obeyed, halting several feet away.

"Come no closer, Demon."

Belthor laughed in his face, shaking his head.

"I am no Demon, First Minister Delnor."

The man balked at the mention of his name, his eyes narrowing as he examined the imposing figure before him, dressed once more in his simple bloodstained robe.

"You have changed since our last Council meeting Delnor. What was it? Fourteen, fifteen years ago?" Before Delnor could reply he was cut off. "Yes, fifteen I would say, only then I thought you were a wise councillor, not the murdering scum you have so obviously become."

Delnor spluttered, his face reddening with rage, "You... You abandoned us in our time of need! You left us and now Demons are among us." He glanced at the crowds of freed prisoners, surrounding the pit in which he, and his men sat.

"Demons eh?" said Belthor quietly, "How can you accuse innocents of being Demons?"

A look of mad triumph flashed in Delnor's eyes. "Our Master, Lord Lailoken, the Changeling, has deemed that the majority of our city has been infiltrated by these Demons, or their familiars. A crusade against evil has begun, and soon an army, the likes of which has not been seen since the times of Ulfner Darkbane, will be gathered and these foul creatures will be banished forever. We have begun the cleansing inquisition and will do as the Changeling Prophecy states and 'Banish the Darkness'. "

Belthor let him rave on, the Changeling Prophecy did indeed state that the Changelings would fly from Darkhaven and banish the darkness, but the Demon that had stolen his son's body now used this prophecy to enforce his will upon the weak minds of the noble families of Darkhaven, stirring up this fanatical fervour of hatred against their fellow city folks.

"Enough, Delnor. Your eyes are clouded by hate and greed. You should have spent more time out in the woods, for you have lost touch with the Goddess. She surely does not reside in your treasure vaults and art collections," Belthor said sadly, before continuing. "The man Lailoken, the one you proclaim Master, is none other than my Son, missing these last fifteen years. He was tainted by the dark teachings of the treacherous Riznar, who's time is short. Now my beloved son is possessed by the Master of Demons, who is seemingly bent on turning man against man, till once again he can claim mastery of this world."

A few of the guards began to rise, frowns of confusion upon their bruised and bloodied faces.

Alvor approached the edge of the pit and waved his rowan staff in a slow arc over his head, mumbling quiet incantations.

Belthor felt a wave of relaxation wash over him, his anger dissolving in a pulse of energy floating down on the ether. Cries of surprise and anger erupted from among the guards, as the dark spells that had tainted their minds slowly sluiced away on the astral wind.

Their anger turned to astonished fear, as they realised in horror the acts they had carried out in the name of a Demon. Most sat back in the mud, sobbing uncontrollably; some just sat and stared into the darkness of their souls; only Lord Delnor stood unmoved.

Belthor looked deep into Delnor's eyes and saw immediately the madness floating behind them, so he raised a hand and slowly stepped towards him, willing to try and heal his troubled mind.

Suddenly Delnor pulled a long, silver dagger from his belt and lunged for Belthor, but his attack stopped abruptly as the point of a thrown spear took him heavily between his shoulder blades, slamming him forwards and knocking him to the mud, face first.

A solemn guard stood empty handed, staring at his dead commander, before he placed his muddy boot on Delnor's back, pulling the spear out with a twist.

A large raven crawed noisily breaking the utter silence. Belthor looked up at the bird perched high in a nearby tree, and nodded to himself, then he looked at the man, a large man with black hair and dark, serious eyes.

"Thank you...Blake," he said.

"No," replied the guard meekly. "Thank you, my Lord."

Belthor frowned, "Just Belthor, son. Just Belthor."

The guard, Blake, looked up at the hundreds of children and old folk. "We cannot return to the city, Belthor."

Belthor closed his eyes for a moment, his head cocked to one side as if listening to something on the breeze.

"Yes." he said, continuing in a voice loud enough for all to hear. "From this day forth, you shall lead the first unit of the Protectors. It will be your duty to escort these people to safety, to the northeast. There in the deep woods you will find the remnants of the Council of Magic. You may well encounter your former inquisitors, and I would expect that they would condemn you very quickly indeed, so I suggest that you do not give them the chance to." Belthor paused as the eyes of every guard bored into him, every face lit with anticipation and hope for redemption.

"Remove these garments of corruption, the Protectors shall wear the plain leather armour with pride. It will be your new uniform."

Blake ripped off his red robe and cast his silver mask aside with disdain, as did every other guard. Now they all stood in their plain tan armour pads.

"Take them northeast into the deep forest, follow my furry friends, they will take you to where the survivors of the Council are in hiding.

"Will you not come with us Belthor?" Blake asked.

Belthor shook his head. "I will not, but my Master, Alvor will follow, masking your passage."

A small blonde boy, of no more than six or seven years pushed his way to the front of the gathered crowd, shouting out in an angry little voice.

"Hey Mister! I want my Mam and Da!"

Belthor looked up at the boy and gave a slight smile. "What is your name, lad?"

"Jack!" he yelled.

Belthor's smile deepened. "What a coincidence, I know a big boy called Jack too! Well, Jack. I promise you this, I will try and find your Mam and Da, but till I do, I want you to take care of all the little boys and girls, for they all probably miss their Mam's and Da's too."

Little Jack's face lit with pride at his important task.

*

As the last of the Guards slipped into the forest taking up a rear defence, Alvor took Belthor by the arm and shook his hand.

"Well Belthor, I cannot say that I envy your journey, or your meetings along the way, but I will make good your promise and return to Darkhaven, and cleanse that plaza, just as soon as we deal with this damn Demon!"

Alvor offered him the rowan staff, "I think you might find this handy."

Belthor hugged his old friend and turned westwards, striking out across the grasslands and the distant river Ulfen.

Chapter 10

Life couldn't be sweeter for Riznar; he sat unopposed at the head of the Council; all his adversaries had fled deep into the forest; and now the last major thorn in his side – Belthor – languished in the cells deep beneath him.

He reclined upon a long padded sofa, his expansive belly spreading freely under his flowing, gold-trimmed, silk robe. Stretching forward with an involuntary grunt, Riznar reached for a plump grape from a solid golden bowl, overflowing with fresh fruit. Popping it into his large mouth, he chomped down and juice poured down his sagging jowls.

For fifty years he had worked to be at this very point, all his dark and devious plans culminated a mere twenty years ago, when he had chosen the young Lailoken to be his apprentice on the 'Path of Shadows'. He was a troubled young man even then; the irony was sweet, for the lad was his adversary's own beloved son.

Lailoken was easily seduced with glimpses of the powers he might attain, then the pair had worked in secret, under Belthor's nose, seeking ways to pierce the Mighty Bind, that held the Demons in the Netherworld.

Riznar burst into gales of high pitched giggles, remembering the night he and Lailoken succeeded in briefly prising open the gate. Strapped and bound tightly to a stone table in Riznar's private rooms, Lailoken had achieved soul-separation, his body linked to his astral form by the familiar silver cord of consciousness.

Riznar had surrounded his prone apprentice with items of power; the black candle; the bell; the chalice of his own precious blood; the dagger, also bloodied; and his own crystal shard, soaked in the blood of several homeless people that his personal guard had abducted from the poor quarters of the city.

After hours of complex ritual and dark incantations, the time was ripe. He smiled as he remembered the terrible screams, for Lailoken had suddenly changed his mind, snapping back into his body as his soul was twinned with the Demonic Master of the Netherworld.

Moments later Lailoken was no more, his young body began to change; eyes sinking into the skull; teeth pushing forwards stretching the skin into a parody of a grin; bones lengthening the muscle and flesh becoming taut and rigid.

The Master had arrived.

Though the Demon was unsure of his surroundings, he recognised instantly the dark magic swirling in the aura of the pathetic being that had freed him from his eternal prison.

Riznar was interrupted from his fond remembrances by a hasty knock on the chamber door. "Enter!" He cried, his high voice echoing around the vaulted ceiling.

An acolyte entered tentatively, limping slightly, his white woollen robes stained red from the blood that still dripped from the chin of his silver face mask.

"Lord Riznar, the prisoner has escaped." His voice was distorted by broken teeth and flattened nose.

Riznar's perfect world began to crack at the edges, and a cold flower of fear blossomed in his guts. "Escaped?" He screamed violently, his pale ice eyes watering, tremors vibrating through the numerous rolls of fat. "You helped him escape, Demon worshipper!" he raved maniacally.

The acolyte took a pace backwards his hands raised in denial, "No, my Lord! They...they attacked me!"

"They? You mean there is more to tell?"

The mask bobbed in a nervous nod, "The old one, Alvor, is free also. They assaulted me, then fled."

"Liar!" Riznar hissed, rising from the settee swifter than his bulk belied. Stalking forwards, he raised a podgy fist and dark fire sprang from his fingertips.

The acolyte gasped, stumbling backwards up till his heels hit the door.

It swung silently open.

Lailoken stood in the doorway, his lifeless eyes radiating deadly menace, though a mask of gold, "So..." He spoke with an unnaturally deep voice, "My adversaries have begun to make moves against me."

Riznar began to sweat, "The assassins have moved in the west, Lord. Even now they seek the Book."

Lailoken's head snapped up and stared directly at Riznar, who suddenly felt weak and insignificant. "The Prophecy still stands, fool. You must go to the river and see that everything proceeds as planned, for if we do not recover the tome soon it will not matter how many of these cattle we cull."

Lailoken lifted the mask from his face, and slowly removed his metallic gloves.

The acolyte gasped, seeing his dark master Lailoken for the first time without the mask or gauntlets of gold. The dark fire died in Riznar's hand, and he reached into the folds of his robes.

Lailoken raised a blackened hand, tendons and bones clearly visible through the patchy, burnt skin. He nodded slowly at Riznar and reached for the doomed man's throat.

The Acolyte's eyes bulged in terror, and he began backing away from the dark-eyed monster before him; right into the vicious thrust of Riznar's dagger point.

The scream echoed through the virtually empty building, and rolled out over a troubled land.

Chapter 11

Jack came groggily awake, wrapped in a thick blanket, beside a roaring fire. He struggled to his elbows, feeling a weary throb in every tendon and muscle. His head pounded and his mouth was parched. Suddenly he was horrified to realise that beneath the blanket he was completely naked.

A waft of cooked meat washed over him and his stomach growled noisily. On the other side of the fire, Samanthiel and the stranger tucked into roast rabbit.

"Sleep well?" She called with a mouthful of meat, "Oh Jack! You need to try this." She waved a bit of meat at him.

"Rabbit?" Jack said, "You've never eaten rabbit before, Sam?"

She shook her head. "Your clothes are over there." She nodded to the saddle hanging on the bough of a tree, with a mischievous twinkle in her eye; his breeks and shirt were draped over the padded leather.

"But...," he stuttered, flushing.

The stranger began to chuckle, his craggy features softened in the firelight. Then he stood, a towering giant of a man, and retrieved Jack's clothing, tossing them to him.

"Thanks," Jack muttered, trying to pull on his undergarments beneath the cover.

"It is you who deserves my thanks, Jack, from this day and forevermore. I would have been feasting now, in the hall of heroes, if I had not stumbled upon your camp."

Samanthiel smiled as Jack finished dressing. "Jack, this is Sigurd Stoneaxe."

Sigurd nodded, dropping to one knee, and Jack frowned.

"Your beautiful companion, has told me of your tremendous accomplishments, my Lord. In my lands a man is judged by his life and his actions. You must be a great sorcerer, to be able to transform into a great, green wyrm."

"Wyrm?" asked Jack.

Sigurd nodded. "Yes, a Dragon I believe you call it."

Jack sat on the log next to Samanthiel, reaching out and pulling some stringy, brown meat from the carcass, stuffing it in his mouth.

Jack noticed the huge axe resting nearby, "Wow, that is some weapon."

Sigurd laughed. "Skullsplitter. He has protected me and my family for centuries, handed down to me from my Father ten years past."

Jack stood, and held his hand out. "Axe," he called imagining a similar weapon to Sigurd's.

In a flash of light, a huge glowing axe appeared magically in his single hand. Sigurd fell backwards in surprise, landing heavily in a pile of dead leaves and moss.

Sigurd rose, eyes wide in wonder, breath held reverently, "Mighty Mother! May I?" he asked holding out his large hands.

Jack balked at the thought of giving up Ulfner Darkbane's magical weapon, then reluctantly he spun the haft and offered it to Sigurd. His hands closed around the smooth handle, and as Jack let go, the weapon slowly dissolved in a shower of small sparks, falling to the forest floor and disappearing.

Samanthiel placed her hand on the hilt of her sword, absently checking it was still there.

Sigurd frowned, picking up Skullspiltter one handed, whirling it noisily. "That is a real axe! Here!"

He handed the thick pole handle to Jack, but he dropped it heavily to the ground. Jack grunted, trying to lift the razor-sharp flint head.

Samanthiel and Sigurd laughed together, before the three returned to their food.

"We must not linger here, Jack. These black hearted men will return and in greater numbers, and I fear that my countrymen will not be able to help us."

Samanthiel frowned, "Why?"

Sigurd's face was changed by a shadow of deep sadness. "My countrymen languish in the deep mines, my lady, prisoners of the Black assassins. A traitor drugged our feasting last week, and the Lord Grim and his warrior band were locked in the abyss."

"Black assassins?" Jack queried with a flutter of fear.

"Garan Snare and his men. He was once a loyal Grimswadian. Now his men feast in our halls, served by our women and children," Sigurd shuddered with suppressed rage. "I must make my way to Ness and seek aid, time is of the essence."

Samanthiel leapt to her feet, whipping her angelic sword from the scabbard. "Snare! He will die, I swear this now."

"Will he now...?" a deep mellow voice sounded from the shadows.

"Sword," cried Jack, crouching ready to attack.

Sigurd spun whipping his axe in a deadly arc, as if it were light as a feather.

A sudden flurry of zips filled the air as several black feathered arrows thunked into the ground at their feet.

"Drop the weapons." The voice demanded in a reasonable, but bored sounding, tone.

The familiar dark figure of Garan Snare appeared from the gloom, flanked by black garbed archers.

Samanthiel hissed, showing her teeth and whilst Sigurd stood tall, almost aloof, his face emotionless.

"Today is a good day to die, Snare," Sigurd said patting his horned helmet into place, rotating the awesome axe.

"I agree," smiled Samanthiel sweetly, Nemesis flashing in the moonlight; she had been on a mission to die fighting Demons, but these black-hearted assassins were top of her list now. "Come dance with me, boys." She leapt high into the air somersaulting right into the middle of the archers.

Jack's sword glowed with a fire of its own, blurring into a deadly attack as he sped for the leader of the assassins, but Sigurd shoulder barged him aside as Snare's weapon sliced the air with deadly accuracy.

Sigurd's axe whistled as he attacked, Garan Snare leapt clear of the arc. Snare flashed a slicing counterattack, but amazingly Sigurd's swift weapon reversal sent the blade skittering along the thick haft, and over balanced the dark assassin.

Jack managed to spy an archer drawing a bead on Samanthiel as she danced her pirouette of death among the rest of the panic-stricken archers.

"Morning Star!" Jack cried whirling the glowing spiked ball at the arm holding the bow. It connected, shattering bone in a miniature explosion of light, the injured man dived into a painful roll, expertly loosing two sharpened throwing-stars. One flew past Jack's left cheek, whilst the other took him high in the right side of his chest, red blossoms staining his white linen shirt.

Samanthiel cried out in rage, pinning the attacker to the earth with the slender point of her sword, leaving him gurgling his last breath, before twisting it savagely and pulling it clear.

Garan Snare dived away from the bite of the flint axe. Leaping high, he grabbed a branch, launching his booted feet into the face of the large axe-wielder. Sigurd fell backwards, his axe dropped. The dark assassin leapt upon him, landing on his chest, effectively immobilising him. As Snare's own slender short sword swept down in a killing stroke, it was met with the clash of divine metal, and the lesser blade shattered.

Samanthiel had dived and rolled thrusting her sword to block the attack, her arm continued back twisting swiftly, changing the defence to counterattack. Nemesis hissed, biting flesh, then only thin air, as Snare back flipped clear.

Snare stood panting heavily, bleeding from the wound on his right arm. Sigurd rose, hefting his axe, and Jack stepped up to join his friends, his shirt now half red.

"Now you die traitor!" Sigurd roared as the three rushed towards him.

Garan Snare's hand moved to the blood ruby at his throat and called, "Home."

As before, the clearing exploded in a flash of blinding energy, and all three were tossed backwards by the tremendous force. This time the energy was not contained within a small room and the effect was lessened, but they were left winded and dazed nonetheless.

Jack staggered to his feet, shaking his head slightly; his ears rang and coloured splotches floated before his eyes. The adrenaline coursing through his blood began to wear off, and a deep, hot pain in his shoulder began to make him feel faint.

"Gods!" Sigurd groaned, sitting up, holding his head.

"Not again!" Samanthiel spat, then she noticed Jack's condition.

Sigurd leapt nimbly to his feet and managed to catch Jack before he fell, he lowered him gently to the ground, next to the fire.

Samanthiel gasped as she pulled Jack's crimson shirt open, revealing a thin semi-circle of spikes, embedded deep in his shoulder. She tentatively reached for the disc.

"Do not pull that!" Sigurd commanded sharply, "He will bleed to death if you do."

Immediately she withdrew her fingers, as Sigurd slung his axe across his back and stooped to pick up Jack, "You carry that saddle and I will carry the boy."

"Where...are...we..." She hoisted the heavy saddle onto her shoulder, "taking...him." Then struggled to draped the bags across her other shoulder.

"We are going to Grimswade, hopefully a physician will still be alive."

Chapter12

For first time in many months Lord Ness slept soundly.

Two days ago, Lupin rode into the city at the head of a column of families, at first Ness had shuddered at the hundreds of new mouths to feed. Then the next day the drovers, shepherds and farmers arrived driving thousands of cattle and sheep. Now, with the city's slaughter houses and butchers working flat out, rationing of food was massively scaled down.

The city had united in thanks, offering their spare rooms to the farmers and their families. After the celebratory feast in their honour, and several pints of the best ale, Ness had settled into his luxurious bed and fallen fast asleep.

But his dreams were troubled...

Ness rode his huge, black war-steed, Thunder, dressed in full battle armour. His ceremonial short sword replaced by his huge, ancient broadsword, strapped diagonally across his back.

The sun blazed in the sky above and sweat dripped from the nose-guard of his helmet. The blasted landscape of dead, twisted trees stretched into the shimmering distance.

His soldiers marched silently behind him, constantly pacing, the trudging tramp of booted foot on hard baked sand, hypnotic.

Suddenly the heat-haze seemed to part and several banners, and flags melted into view. Ness raised his gauntlet covered fist, and his men halted instantly. A party of men rode into the near distance and drew to a stop, banners fluttering noisily in the stiffening breeze.

Ness stared hard through narrowing eyes, squinting through the dazzling sun at the banners, then he realised that they were the red star on a white background; the emblem of Darkhaven.

He clicked his tongue, and gave a gently prod with his heels, Thunder took off at a swift trot towards the waiting entourage.

As he drew nearer, he recognised six of the seven Tower-lords from the sunken city of Ulfenspan, along with two strangers wearing red robes and metal masks; one silver, one gold.

"Halt! Demon." A shrill, but familiar voice rang out from behind the silver mask.

Ness pulled on the reins, bringing Thunder to a prancing halt. He lifted off his heavy helmet, placing it upon the pommel of the saddle, running his fingers through his thick, grey hair, his noble brow darkening in confusion.

"The Inquisition has judged and found you guilty of consorting with Demons."

"Are you insane?" Ness cried angrily, turning in his saddle, "We have battled the Demons and defeated them at Ness, and since then in the surrounding countryside!"

But as he spoke his defence, his troops began to change, to transform before his eyes, into a rippling wave of twisting and jerking limbs. His own men had become a rabble of slavering monsters, roaring and moaning and gnashing their shark-like teeth.

Ness screamed, as the Demons broke into a mad run...

He woke screaming on sweat-stained sheets, moonlight flooding the room from the deep bay window. A soft creak sounded as a guard stood silhouetted at the foot of his four poster bed.

"Are you troubled, my Lord?" he asked in a loud whisper.

"Water...please pass me a drink of water."

He drank deeply from the silver tankard, before passing the empty container to the patient guard.

"Anything else, Sir?"

Ness waved him away, "I am fine, please forgive my nightmares; too much beer."

He lay panting, deeply relieved that it was a mere dream. As his racing heart began to slow and his breath deepen, he began to feel a presence in the room. Trying not to overreact he deliberately slowed his breathing further, circulating his breath, feeling the energy flowing through his room. Then he began to try and sense the presence.

Immediately he got the feeling of his old friend Belthor.

His heart sank, thinking *Is Bethor in the world of Spirit?*

A familiar deep voice echoed in his inner ear, as if from a great distance, "No... not... dead... dead... dead. Dream... is... a... warning... Lailoken... and... Riznar... coming ...for ...you...you ...you."

Ness gave a mental nod, a deep dread sinking in his heart, almost pressing him into the soft mattress. Then, as quick as it had appeared, the presence diminished and faded completely. Ness had the gist of what was to be done.

His heart raced, and his old muscles tightened in antici-pation, as he swept the blankets off, and rose from the bed, lighting the wick of his table lantern. Instantly the door burst open, the solid looking guard with his sword drawn, leapt into the room, ready to fight; security had been tightened ever since the criminal Harry the Crow, possessed by a demon, had leapt through the window and kidnapped a warlock.

Ness almost leapt out of his skin, but gave the guard a grim smile nonetheless. "Summon Captain Reed, and the housemen," he ordered, and as the man snapped a smart salute. "Oh, and send someone out into the forest to search for the lad Lupin."

*

Less than an hour later, his official dining hall was filled with tired, grim-faced men all smartly turned out, despite the hour and the night's celebrations. All except Lupin, who had been off running with his pack of brothers and sister, and now sat wearing only a hastily pulled on pair of ill-fitting breeks and a baggy shirt, loaned by the guard that found him.

A roaring fire crackled and spat in the hearth, as the men settled around the meeting table.

"Thank you for the prompt gathering gents," Ness began. "I have received troubling news, by way of an ill omen."

His men sat poker-straight, their attention razor sharp, for most knew of their Lord's magical abilities, and none had any shadow of doubt in their hearts at his warning.

Lupin nodded, his dark eyes reflecting the firelight, he interrupted, "My Father Belthor sent me a warning also, Lord Ness. He has told me terrible news from Darkhaven."
All heads turned to the young man. "It seems that the Demon possessing my Brother, Lailoken, and the fat councillor Riznar, have overthrown the Magic Council, killing many. Darkhaven is in chaos, fear and hate are ravaging the streets."

"With Ulfenspan gone, help is impossible" Captain Reed said.

"Help," Ness said slowly, "...is not going to be the issue here, Reed. You see, Belthor has indicated that the Demon and Riznar are coming here, to Ness and they will not be coming alone..."

A rumble of murmurs swept around the table, before Lupin stood and placed his palms on the tabletop, all eyes returned to him.

"I will rejoin my pack and skirt the Ulfen, we will scout from the Giant's Teeth, all the way to the sea. I will return when we discover more."

Chapter 13

Belthor stood on a rocky outcrop, gripping the rough crystalline stone with a gnarled hand. The panoramic view from the hilltop, sloping down towards the distant river Ulfen, shook him to the core. Once a mighty forest of ancient trees grew among these gentle hills, it had been a place he used to lose himself for days, in times less troubled. Now the landscape was stippled by thousands of stumps and holes, where trees were hacked down, or literally torn from the rich, dark earth.

The grasslands skirting the riverside were now covered in a blanket of humanity, the army Delnor spoke of was tented there, in their thousands.

The dying afternoon sun stained the river blood-red, running from the north to the south for over a thousand miles to the sea, the river Ulfen split the land.

It had been rendered impassable by Belthor's own hand, when he destroyed the river-city of Ulfenspan, on the express command of the Council. Belthor now knew that this must have been part of Riznar's plan all along.

But the destruction of the forest troubled him more, for trees were a tremendous source of magic; their roots spreading the energy from the Goddess below, and their leaves converting astral energy from the heavens to feed the land. He could feel a deep sadness radiating from the wounded land, and as a small squirrel darted to-and-fro among the stumps desperately searching for food, a single tear ran down his ruddy cheek into his beard.

The rowan staff began to pulsate softly in Belthor's fist as he made his way slowly northwards along the ridge, through the stumps and holes fringed with torn roots. As he crested the next hill his knees folded involuntarily and he retched noisily amongst the fallen leaves, his head swimming with a throbbing pain.

He leaned heavily on the staff, whispering a swift ritual, using its inner energy to create a sphere of protection around him. Instantly he regained some strength and well-being, and stood straight again.

Belthor squinted in the dying light, up ahead something regularly pulsed red, lighting up the darkening sky to the north. He knew instinctively that the flashing light must be the source of the trouble, and he picked up his pace.

Despite the chill of nightfall, he wiped a sheen of sweat from his bald head and brow, as he trudged up the small hill. The light grew in intensity with each step he took, and a very low vibration thrummed in the air, setting his teeth on edge.

Belthor crouched as he approached the crest of the hill, peering cautiously into the valley below.

A long line of chained people were being funnelled into a bottleneck at the mouth of the valley. The guards separated a group of twenty or more prisoners, herding them into the middle of a large circle of jagged standing stones.

Lightning danced between the obelisks, as dozens of red robed figures linked hands around the stone circle. The buzzing grew louder, setting Belthor's teeth chattering, and a large swirling blob of darkness formed above the cowering captives.

Belthor gripped the staff tighter, gritting his teeth painfully, as the ball lowered and enveloped the wailing people. The hemisphere pulsed with a bright, luminous, light and began to shrink, slowly forming a bizarre new shape. The captives in the centre of the circle had been transformed into a single abominable amalgamation of rock and flesh, hulking and hideous, vaguely humanoid, but on a massive scale. One huge squat head with burning coal eyes built into a torso of rock; two thick arms ended in mighty stone hammers; but worst of all, the faces of all the captives were etched into the stone body, each twisted in terror and agony.

The amalgam creature swayed in the centre of the circle, its hammers, each the size of a fully grown man, nearly touched the ground. A red robed mage stepped into the circle, striking the beast with a staff tipped with a silver eagle. Light flared and died, and the monstrosity turned slowly, lumbering on tree-trunk legs through the circle and into a huge cave mouth.

The red mage rejoined his brothers and the next group of captives were beginning to be pushed forwards.

Belthor stood and raised his staff skywards, swirling it in a wide circle, before pointing it to the East and intoning one of the secret names of the Creator, "**Yohevahe**."

A stiff wind sprang up from the still sky.

He turned southwards and pointed towards the distant sea and called out, "**Adonai**."

Another stronger wind gusted, sweeping in dark storm-clouds. Thunder cracked and a spear of bright lightning lanced between the dark clouds.

Whirling the staff Westwards he cried out, "**Eheieh**."

His beard and robes flapped wildly in the stronger winds that now began to brew, churning the sky.

He stabbed the staff Northwards, crying, "**Agla**."

A bitter wind, directly from the Giant's Teeth, gusted violently. Finally he planted the staff into the earth, crying out in a deep power-filled voice, "**Amen**."

The winds buffeted Belthor left and right, almost tossing him into the valley. The sky boiled and churned and Belthor fell to his knees as a giant finger of swirling clouds, lanced downwards into the valley, sweeping the stone circle with screaming ferocity. The red robed mages clung to the stones desperately, as several of their brethren vanished into the churning darkness.

The chained captives clung to each other for stability; the sheer weight of their number saved them from the ravages of the tornado.

Suddenly a glow of crackling energy formed above the standing stones, and shot into the middle of the clouds. Lightning lit the swirling vortex, then a tremendous explosion smashed the cyclone, sending the four winds back to the corners of the world.

A dead calm settled over the scene and Bethor knew instantly that he was in deep trouble. He ducked and scrambled back over the top of the hill. Suddenly the ground beside him erupted, and gouts of flame and earth shot skywards, tossing him into the air like an oversized rag doll.

Chapter 14

Grimswade sprawled on the south side of the last mountain in a ridge of high snow-capped peaks; a tumbling cascade of square stone buildings, seemingly built one upon the other and connected by a maze of narrow roads and alleyways.

Sigurd and Samanthiel moved silently through the dark city. They had spent hours marching through the dense forest, struggling with their burdens, before finally reaching the cleared and tilled slopes of the foothills.

Samanthiel's thighs burned as she sweated beneath the heavy saddle and bags. *How many steps are in this damned city!* She cursed silently, huffing as they began another crooked flight of stairs between two dark buildings.

"Not much further, my lady," Sigurd whispered, not even breaking sweat, as he cradled Jack easily in his untiring arms.

Nobody walked the streets or alleyways, although curtains twitched surreptitiously in darkened windows, and swiftly closed shutters greeted their passing.

Halfway up the steps, Sigurd stopped and turned to a dark alcove, before gently rapping on a door. Samanthiel stopped at his side, glancing warily past him, up the steps into the gloom, and back down from where they had come.

Sigurd repeated the gentle knock, as a faint glow seemed to grow in the main street below. A single figure approached, ascending the steps slowly but steadily, a heavily shuttered lantern only lighting the immediate area. Samanthiel rested the saddle gently on the flagstone paving, and placed a hand on the hilt of her sword, pulling Nemesis silently from the scabbard.

The figure was wrapped in black from head to toe, and carried a crooked staff of old wood. Sigurd turned, one hand on the handle of his stone axe.

"Put your weapon away, child. I mean you no harm." A female voice spoke, slightly muffled through the cloth. The dark woman pushed past Sigurd and placed a slender hand upon the black painted door.

"Open."

The door swung silently inwards.

She stepped across the threshold and beckoned them in. Sigurd followed immediately and Samanthiel checked up and down the lane, before following, and closing the heavy door.

The dark room was sparsely furnished. A solid table with a few crude chairs sat in the middle of the room. The room was tiny with an open hearth, hanging griddle and pothook. A heavy dark-wood chest sat on the right of the fireplace and a simple box-bed was built into the wall on the left.

Sigurd had to stoop to avoid hitting his head on the thick, blackened roof beams, as the woman walked to the hearth and hissed a whisper.

Small flames burst into life among the logs, casting crazy orange and black shadows around the room.

He bent low and placed Jack upon the table, unwrapping the heavy cloak from around him. Samanthiel gasped as she saw his face; he was deathly pale and breathing shallowly.

The woman in black shrugged off her cloak, revealing a tall, middle-aged woman, hatchet-faced with raven hair tumbling wildly over thin shoulders. Her piercing black eyes gave her the look of a crow, but she radiated an air of authority and confidence.

She looked from Sigurd, to Jack then back to Sigurd again, "My Lord, you risk too much returning to the city."

My Lord?...Samanthiel frowned, looking hard at Sigurd.

"Mistress Inga, please help my young friend. We will talk later of risks."

Samanthiel took hold of Jack's hand, it was cold and clammy.

Mistress Inga whipped around, snapping, "Don't touch him, girl!"

Samanthiel instantly let go of the hand. "I'm sorry...I," she stumbled through an apology as Inga lifted down a bundle of twigs, hanging from the rafters above the fireplace. She untied the twine and hunched down on the floor. "Silence..." She hissed in a low voice.

From the folds of her clothing she produced a slim, dark bladed dagger, whispering a ritual, and etching the air with a pentangle. Reaching into the fireplace, she wafted handfuls of smoke over her face, before picking up the bundle of twigs and casting them over the floor.

Inga sat still for a moment gazing over the confused mess of fallen wood, then she began to chant, murmuring in a low voice, palms raised to the roof.

Samanthiel gave a small gasp as two small flames appeared to dance in Inga's cupped hands. She slowly rose to her feet, arms outstretched, "Open the shirt," she barked a command.

Samanthiel and Sigurd pulled Jack's bloody shirt open, exposing the jagged semi-circle buried deep in his chest. Inga slowly lowered her burning hands and cupped them over the wound. Instantly Jack began to tremble. A shimmer of scales swept up and down his chest, swirling over his abdomen before sinking beneath his skin. He groaned, smoke rising between his gritted teeth.

"Elgor's Eye!" Sigurd exclaimed.

Samanthiel had seen something similar when Lupin had been injured by a Demon, but her pulse raced nonetheless.

Inga began to breath deeply, her arms vibrated violently and her hair was plastered to her shining forehead.

"Never...," she gasped, hoarsely, "have I felt power like this..."

Sigurd rushed to steady her, and was virtually pushed from his feet as a flash of light exploded from Jack's chest. Inga screamed collapsing to her knees, amazingly her hands were still cupped in position.

"It is done!" She cried, holding up a silver circle in one trembling hand. "The Valkyries will not be claiming his soul this night."

Samanthiel peered at Jack's chest; nothing remained but a thin whitened line on his bloody chest.

Jack moaned and opened his eyes, looking directly into Samanthiel's. "I had a strange dream, Sam," he said distantly, "I had a big crow on my chest pecking at me. It had feet of fire and a razor sharp beak."

Inga chuckled throatily, "They do call me - The Moors Crow."

Jack turned his head, seeing Inga being helped to her feet by Sigurd. "Forgive me..." Jack stammered.

Inga shook her head with a smile, "An apology is not needed."

"He is a Dragon Changeling, Lady Inga." Samanthiel explained.

"Yes, Mistress Inga. He is a mighty wyrm, I swear by Elgor's all seeing eye."

Inga arched a thick eyebrow, frowning, "I never thought I would live to see this day. Many, many years ago, my mistress told me of the Changelings in the Haunted Forest. It is said that a Green Mother lives there with her children."

"Children?" Jack interrupted, pushing himself up onto his elbows. "What is the Green Mother's name?"

"Patience, young Changeling," she chided, before continuing. "My Mistress learned her Witchlore in the deep woods around the time of my Great Grandmother. She lived to the North of here, on the edge of a swampy forest, a dark and forbidding place. My Mistress used to talk of the Green Lady; the Changeling Guardian of the Haunted Woods; Mother of the shapeless ones; Keeper of the sacred grove," She paused as her audience hung upon her every word, "My Mistress called her Gaia."

Chapter 15

"My Lord Alvor!" One of the rear guard soldiers cried out in the distance.

Alvor tutted a quiet complaint to himself and left the front of the column of refugees and troops, making his way back to the end of the line.

Half a dozen of the Protectors took up the rear, trying in vain to mask the trail of the hundreds passing through the darkened woodland.

A young soldier in simple leather armour, ran up to him, panting breathlessly. "My...Lord...There is movement behind us, we are being followed."

Alvor stopped and glanced back at the snake of torches disappearing between the trunks of the giant trees.

"Right Lad, run to the front and get everyone to douse the torches, then tell your commander to take half of the men back here, and the rest must try as best they can to get old and young further away from here."

The soldier nodded and disappeared into the gloom.

Alvor nodded to himself in satisfaction as the line of torches slowly were extinguished, one by one. Moving closer to the rear guard, he spoke softly to the men.

"Please sit still and guard my body a moment, I am going to try something."

The guards formed a loose circle, weapons drawn, as the old man sat cross-legged, with his back to a mighty oak.

Alvor slowed his breathing and closed his eyes, feeling the tremendous power flowing through the ancient tree. The energy seeped through the rough bark into his body, lifting his spirit high with the rush of power. Moments later Alvor's spirit floated above his physical body.

He turned his attention back the way they had travelled. Bright green pulses of light swirled outwards from each tree, spiralling up into the sky like sparks from a large bonfire; lighting the forest brighter than day. Suddenly he caught glimpses of colour flashing between the trees; the multi-coloured living lights of human aura.

They were right, he thought to himself, as more colours flickered off to the left and right. It seemed they were vastly outnumbered. He made himself float higher, above the treetops, then recoiled in horror; several pulsing red orbs floated in the distance, bobbing and weaving between the boughs and branches.

Soul Seekers! Alvor cursed, instantly raising a mental shield around his astral body.

A Soul Seeker spell was notoriously hard to conjure and even harder to control, the bright spheres would track the human aura, sending the information back via a mindlink to the person that created them; it meant that their pursuers had to include three or even four high ranking wizards or sorcerers.

Alvor swept back down into his body, returning from the weightlessness of his spirit-form always made him feel woozy and heavy. He pushed himself upright, discovering that he was now encircled by Blake and most of the Protectors.

"Gather round." Alvor whispered, as the sounds of men trampling the forest undergrowth filled the night.

With weapons drawn, the Protectors huddled close to the old wizard, who began to whisper a swift spell of concealment, followed by a mantra chant that began to channel the earth power from the surrounding forest, deep into the soil and up through the soles of his feet. He felt the energy build, and the small hairs all over his body stood erect. Blake and his men stared in wonder as the old wizard began to shimmer and vibrate, luminous lines of pure power snaking beneath his skin.

Alvor could sense the red orbs floating overhead, pulsing out a warning too late, for it was then that he raised his glowing hand and pressed it against the bark of a tree.

A rush of power shot up through the tree, into the air and filled the red orbs with an overload of directed energy. The glowing globes swelled and exploded soundlessly in the night sky, shattering the mindlink and sending a deep burning pain into the mind's of their creators.

A distant commotion filled the night with wailing cries of pain and anger, but by now the sound of men approaching seemed to come from everywhere.

Alvor took a deep breath and placed his hand on Blake's shoulder. "Well Blake, it is time to earn your promotion."

Blake nodded giving silent hand signals to his men. They spread into a semicircle around Alvor, who had picked up a stout branch.

As the first red cloaks came into sight, Blake raised his sword high. "PROTECTORS, CHARGE!"

The leather clad warriors leapt into action, striking with swift deadly accuracy, cutting down the red-cloaks before they knew just what had happened to them. The chasing guards had expected an easy night rounding up the escaping children and old folk, but instead they now faced the armed defence of professional soldiers and an angry wizard.

The co-ordination of the pursuing guards was thrown into confused disarray, as the ring of steel on steel and cries of the wounded filled the darkness. The fight fell to hand-to-hand, single combat and soon the bodies of the fallen red-cloaks began to include several of the protectors. The enemy grew stronger with each charge, but now they withdrew and regrouped, ready to concentrate their attack.

Alvor clung to a tree, gasping for breath and bleeding from a deep gash on his head. He felt calm and happy in the knowledge that the refugees were escaping deeper into the forest.

Blake was uninjured, the only man to be so; most of the surviving men were cut, bloodied and bruised, but none complained.

Then the a tree exploded into a shower of fiery sparks and splinters, as the enemy wizards regained their strength.

Alvor pushed himself upright. "Men of Darkhaven!" he shouted into the night. "Hear me now. If the Great Goddess Danu wills it, I will die here this night in her dark wood, not by the will of the Demon Lailoken."

"Silence, Demon!" a voice shouted nearby, but there seemed to be a clamour of confusion within the enemy ranks.

Alvor could hear someone shout in the distance. "He said the name of the Goddess!"

Then another shouted. "They cannot be Demons."

Suddenly a loud tearing filled the night, followed by a flash.

Lines of brilliance formed a massive web of light that hung in the air between two trees. It split in two and separated like a doorway, revealing a gigantic green figure bathed in a glorious golden light. He was easily as tall as three men, and covered from head to toe in leaves, vines and grasses, sporting a massive pair of many tined antlers.

"Who dares destroy my forest?" a deep elemental voice cried passionately.

Chapter 16

The wide double doors swung soundlessly open, and Garan Snare swept into the chamber for the second time in as many weeks. Blood dripped slowly and regularly from his fingertips, staining the expensive red carpet with a line of darker dots.

A massive oval, stone table filled the centre of the room. It had a mirror smooth surface that seemed to swirl and boil like clouds in a storm. Something appeared to twinkle and shine deep within the surface, and as he passed, Snare touched the tabletop, leaving a bloody fingerprint. The blood hissed and sizzled, and for a few moments the clouds parted, revealing a twilight map of Darkhaven and the surrounding lands all in miniature, as if viewed from a tremendous height.

His wonder was broken by a metallic gurgling laugh. At the head of the table sat Lailoken; his paymaster. Snare felt something unsettling tugging at his guts, twisting them with what could only be described as fear; a long forgotten experience for the assassin.

Lailoken lounged on a golden throne, one leg draped lazily over the thick shining arm. His mask reflected the light making it glow as if his face was on fire. He regarded the assassin approaching, sensing the growing apprehension in the other man. His dead eyes widened at the sight and smell of the blood, and he rose instantly from his seat.

"Ahh Snare. You are injured," Lailoken said with a metallic hiss, raising a beckoning hand. "Come closer, let me... look at this...for you."

Garan Snare stopped a little beyond arm's reach, his heart beating wildly. He knew that his paymaster was a sorcerer of high power, and that it would be foolish to disobey, but he possessed magical charms and talismans that would negate his orders.

Lailoken gave another deep gurgling laugh, "You think to disobey me, assassin?" He raised his gloved hand and gave a twisting gesture. The magical devices pinned to his cloak began to glow, the twists of hair and tiny shards of bone disintegrating and falling to pieces, littering the carpet.

Garan Snare quickly raised his hand to his throat and felt reassured that the Blood Ruby was still intact, but suddenly he felt compelled to drop his cloak on the floor. He loosened the cords and it fell heavily, the concealed weapons clinking with a muffled thud.

The open wound on his arm sent a pulse of blood running down to his fingers. Lailoken took hold of his wrist and raised the bloody hand to his mask, inhaling deeply. Garan snare looked through the mask and did not like the eyes that he met there.

Lailoken tightened his grip painfully and forced Snare's hand to press against the seeing table. The surface cleared again, the heat searing the palm of his hand, as it spat and hissed like a frying pan full of sausages.

"You see the clouds to the northwest?" he asked the struggling assassin. "That is the mage, Belthor, and off to the northeast, that commotion in the woods is his mentor Alvor and some of my prisoners..."

He let Snare pull his hand clear of the hot surface, his palm blistered and raw.

Lailoken gave another throaty gurgle, as he pulled off his glove. His own hand was blackened and burnt, tendons and muscles fried when he and the Demon possessed 'Harry the Crow' had pulled the magical defences from the ground at Ness.

As he opened and closed his fist, small pieces of charred and stinking flesh crackled and fell to the red carpet. He placed the almost skeletal hand on the wounded shoulder and instantly a freezing pain shot through the assassin. He fought to remain conscious, as the flesh on his arm froze then burned in rapid succession. When Lailoken removed his hand it had regenerated some of the flesh, and the wound was now replaced by a livid red scar in the shape of a thin hand.

"Yes Snare, my enemies are at large. But it does not trouble me overly much, for soon you will retrieve the Angel's book for me."

Snare knew that the Book was hidden deep in a Haunted Forest, protected by magic. Compared to the creature Lailoken, the ghosts in the woods paled into insignificance.

"You shall be sent to the southern borders of these woodlands, for my magic cannot penetrate the fogs and mists from here."

Garan Snare spoke up. "My men are in Grimswade. I need to go there. Lord Grim's son has returned..."

"You will go alone!" Lailoken interrupted. "Your men are able to care for themselves, is...that... clear?" He finished in a threatening whisper.

Snare nodded, eyes slits. He would take great satisfaction slitting this wizard's throat.

Lailoken roared out in laughter. "You cannot kill me human!" He pulled the mask from his face and let Garan Snare see the face of death. "You see me Garan Snare, and I see you..."

Lailoken gripped Garan Snare by the throat, lifting him with one powerful arm, before slamming him onto the table. "Go!"

The magical power coursed though the blood ruby and the table, and in a bright flash the assassin was gone.

Chapter 17

Jack and Samanthiel looked at each other.

"Gaia!" exclaimed Jack.

"Belthor's Sister!" cried Samanthiel.

Mistress Inga frowned, "I do not know this Belthor, but the tales of Gaia and her offspring have been used to scare young around here, since before I was born."

Jack told her of Garan Snare; the abduction of Belthor; the Demonic Lailoken; and their urgent quest to seek out Gaia and the Book of Raziel.

"It seems Garan Snare has made many enemies across the lands, and you have become embroiled in a deadly game of cat and rat. I think you need to leave Grimswade before the sun rises, this tome that you seek is not unknown to the Hidden Sisterhood, and if Snare and his men are seeking it..."

She let the dire consequences hang in the air.

Jack shook his head. "We will help Sigurd, before continuing for the book," he declared, Samanthiel nodding her agreement.

Mistress Inga stood up, reaching for Sigurd, "Come, we need to talk...alone."

Sigurd shook his grizzled head. "Speak openly Mistress. These friends are to be trusted."

Inga sighed, and sat again. "Very well, Sigurd. I know that you were out hunting when the treacherous Garan Snare and his dogs arrived. You know that he has imprisoned the warband in the deep mines. But...you need to know that your Father was slain, Sigurd. He was killed before the court," She paused and wiped a tear, sniffing loudly. "He died *without* a sword in his hand Sigurd...and they took his head."

Sigurd moaned, slamming a fist noisily against the table, tears of rage coursing down his scarred face. Grimswadians believed that the Hall of Heroes was only available to those that died honourably in battle or with cold, sharp steel in their hand.

Samanthiel swallowed hard, biting back her tears, the memory of her lost family still burned bright and painful. Suddenly she felt a strange feeling in her head, as if something called to her from a great distance. Frowning, she cocked her head, straining to hear.

Mistress Inga spotted the strange look in the girl's eyes, and placed a hand on Sigurd's thick forearm. "Hush my Lord...A spirit is moving among us..."

She looked at Jack, gave a small secretive smile, then nodded to someone or something lurking in the dark shadows.

Jack relaxed deeply and felt strangely sleepy, but also wide awake at the same time. His breath deepened, and his chin slowly fell to his chest as his body fell into a trance. Gradually a presence filtered into his mind, a warm feeling of sparkling energy rushed up his spine into the back of his head, no threat seemed to present itself, so Jack welcomed the spirit silently.

Mistress Inga linked hands with Jack and Sigurd, and Samanthiel instinctively followed suit.

"Come forth spirit, we welcome you to the physical plane, join our circle of love and light." Inga intoned ritually.

Jack slowly sat tall with his eyes closed, and his back straight and stiff. His mouth formed into a wide, low frown with jutting chin, and his voice deepened to that of an old man.

"Sigurd...take heed..." A freezing chill swept around the room as the spirit began to communicate.

"Father?" He recognised the lilt of his voice, and the expressions etched into Jack's young face.

"LISTEN!" Jack roared, eyes still shut. "You can save my men, Sigurd. They languish in the deep mine. There is a secret entrance...through the bottom of the dungeons, the old well beyond the guardroom...get them out!"

"I will, Father." Sigurd whispered humbly, his voice breaking.

The temperature rose and a feeling of well-being filled the circle.

"Fear not, Sigurd. For I do not wander the 'Plain of Lost Souls'; I have been reunited with my ancestors, and I will watch over you till the day we can feast together in the Hall of Heroes..."

The voice was thick with emotion, and a single tear fell from Jack's closed eyes.

Samanthiel felt Nemesis vibrating and heating in the scabbard against her leg, so she broke the circle and reached down to touch the pommel. The sword lent her second sight, and the glowing outline of a man standing beside Jack melted into view, he seemed to be reaching out to touch her weapon.

"Ah, truly a weapon worthy of the Queen of Swords." Lord Grim spoke through Jack again.

Samanthiel smiled. "Thank you. It was gifted to me by the Archangel Michael, my Lord."

Jack shook his head slowly. "No, my dear. Sigurd is now the Lord of Grimswade, I am merely a shade, drifting back into this plane to help his son. Now I will return to my rest, please make haste...all of you."

Jack slumped forwards and hit his head on the table, instantly coming awake.

"Ow! I am sorry, did I fall asleep?" he apologised.

"You channelled the spirit of Lord Grim, and he told us some useful things." Samanthiel said blinking away the vision of the ghost.

Sigurd swept Jack up in his arms and gave him a huge bear hug, roaring with joy. Jack wheezed in the tight grasp, confused and amazed in equal measure.

*

They left Inga's humble dwelling, moving swiftly further up the winding alleyway. The witch had prepared several small bottles of coloured liquid, which she had tucked into pockets of her midnight cloak.

As they approached the Castle, Inga motioned them quietly into a darker alley and slipped a small red bottle from her pocket. Opening the stopper with a pop, she poured the liquid into a puddle on the flagstone path.

She crouched low, breathing and whispering quiet incantations, performing strange finger-motions and giving clicks of her tongue, before touching the shining surface with her hazel wand. The puddle began glowing and bubbling, hissing and steaming, the smoke rising and forming a shape in the air.

Samanthiel and Jack watched entranced as the smoke gathered, swirling and churning, solidifying into the crude likeness of a small, red Dragon.

"Fly, Shadow-wyrm. Cause mayhem and terror, lead them a merry dance!" Inga commanded the shining simulacrum.

The insubstantial Dragon seemed to take on an intelligence and flapped leathery wings, soaring high into the night before swooping down and vanishing over the wall. Moments later shouts went up, cries of alarm and anger, which receded into the distance.

"Come, we must hurry, for the Shadow-wyrm will only live for moments longer." Inga called as she made her way to the unguarded gate.

As they passed into the shadow of the main gate, Jack heard Sigurd gasp and begin shuddering quietly beside him in the darkness. He simply stood staring upwards at his Father's grisly head impaled on a pike above the portcullis.

"Garan Snare... Elgor's Ravens will strip your flesh on the endless 'Plains of the Lost' for all eternity. This I swear." He whispered, making the horned finger oath.

"He will, Sigurd." Jack said, placing a hand on the man's trembling shoulder.

"Come, my Lord, time is short." Inga whispered, pulling gently on Sigurd's arm, leading them across the courtyard to the doorway to the dungeons.

The narrow spiral stairway opened out into an empty guard room, it stank of sweat and old blood; the dark stains still colouring the rough flagstone floor. The walls were lined with racks of short throwing spears; long handled axes, short and long swords; all well cleaned and oiled.

"Nice swords," said Samanthiel, running her hand along the hilts of the shining weapons appreciatively.

"Grimswadian steel, the best in the world." Sigurd declared proudly. The deep mines below the city were rich in iron ore and the metallurgists and smiths worked hand in hand to produce the finest blades.

"In the mists of time, a hot rock of pure iron fell from the skies. It is said that the God Elgor found the stone and from it, made a sword unlike any made since..." Mistress Inga began.

"Like this?" interrupted Jack, holding up his hand and calling, "Sword."

The fiery blade sprang into his hand from nowhere, startling the witch, reflecting in the array of metalwork around the room.

"Darkbane's sword...," she whispered in awe, reaching out to touch the cool blue flames. "Yet again you surprise me, young Changeling."

Sigurd grunted as he lifted the heavy wooden bar from the single door to the cells. "Come, we will compare swords when my men are free!" he said, pushing open the iron bound door.

The corridor was pitch black, and Jack led the way, the light from his drawn sword enough to see by. The cells were empty, and surprisingly clean. At the end of the passage the floor ended in a wide hole, with a large pulley suspended from the roof beam, and a thick rope disappearing down into the inky dark.

Chapter 18

A nimbus of tiny green lights swirled in the darkness, forming and reforming the shape of the giant horned man, his piercing gaze sweeping back and forth between the two parties of men.

"Be still." The voice of the green man was filled with power and deep sadness.

The woodland fell silent, the cries of the dying and wounded soldiers ceased, every single living thing stopped.

Alvor slumped exhausted against the tree, surrounded by the last of the Protectors. Ahead, red cloaked soldiers stood immobile, weapons dropped and forgotten.

"My trees," he began in a dolefully deep voice, sweeping a leafy hand between the boughs of the surrounding treetops. **"Ah, they weep. Can you not feel it? The pain? The loss? I feel it. Yes, you humans come here and destroy, burn, cut and kill."**

Alvor rose shakily, wiping his bloodied face on the sleeve of his robes. "My Lord Cerranos, we have not come here intending harm, we flee, seeking the safety of the deep woods."

The Green man gazed down with burning eyes, **"Death is your companion, man of earth, and destruction your shadow. Your dark magic corrupts the lands to the west, killing my trees and sapping the goodness from the land."**

He shook his head slowly, casting his gaze on the pile of wounded and dying men, **"Why must you men of earth harm each other?"**

He turned to the gathered attackers. **"Why..."** he paused and took several deep sniffs that rustled the leaves in the surrounding trees. **"I smell the taint of the Dark One. He holds sway over the hearts and minds of your**

leaders, and grows more powerful with every act of evil done in the name of good. I sense him… watching…"

One by one, the enemy dropped to their knees, heads lowered in shame. A mage dropped his red cloak and silver mask, tossing his staff aside in disgust, before calling out to Lord Cerranos in a trembling voice.

"My Lord, Please forgive our ignorance. We have been blinded by hatred and evil. We do not deserve mercy…but beg it."

The Green man nodded, and closed his leafy eyes. He raised his long arms high into the air, and began to sway back and forth like a tree in a storm. Slowly he began to dissolve, returning to tiny sparks of luminescent green. The glowing flecks fluttered and floated downwards, swirling and joining others in miniature whirlwinds of light, each reforming into more than a dozen man-sized green beings, pulsing with an inner light.

They moved among the soldiers and Protectors, placing bright hands on the shoulder of each man. One moved close to Alvor and reached up to place a cool, healing hand on his wounded head. A wave of peace swept through him, rejuvenating energy coursing through his body, replacing every ache and pain.

"Thank you," he said simply, tears forming in his eyes.

"You have been healed," the same soulful voice echoed from all the figures simultaneously.

On the ground, each of the wounded men slowly sat up, untangling arms and legs, their wounds miraculously healed.

Thinking to repay the kind gesture, Alvor reached out and placed a hand on the shining shoulder of the nearest green being, drawing up a charge of earth energy through his feet and it sending through his hand into the figure.

Alvor removed his hand and was amazed to see a shining handprint on the glowing green skin. Bright tendrils snaked and radiated out from the print's fingertips, spreading and turning the figure from green to a soft golden.

All the glowing figures turned simultaneously, reached out, touching their colourful companion. The glow passed down each outstretched arm in a chain reaction of light, till all shared the new colour.

The figures began to pulse brighter for a moment before exploding soundlessly into fragments of swirling light, then re-forming into the horned giant once again.

"Ahh...many aeons have passed since I have shared the power of my Sister Danu...You have taught me a valuable lesson, Alvor of the Earth Goddess; not all men of earth grow in the darkness, and once the shadow has been lifted, the light within is pure and good."

"My Lord, we are seeking a hidden enclave of our brethren within these woods; they are refugees of the terrible times the Demon Master has imposed on our city."

Lord Cerranos glowed golden for a few more moments, before returning to his natural green. He raised one leafy arm and pointed above the trees, into the dark clouds high above; a lance of green light shot skywards, momentarily turning night to day, then fading to black.

"It is done," he nodded with a solemn smile. **"His eye has been temporarily blinded; whilst you remain within this woodland your passage will remain hidden and no taint from the Dark One can influence you."**

Mobility returned to the soldiers and the two parties met and embraced, reunited as brothers once again.

Lord Cerranos nodded his approval and addressed the new company of troops and wizards, **"In times long past, I aided my Sister and her champion, Ulfner Darkbane, in the creation of the Netherworld. Now the Demon seeks to destroy all life on this plane. "**

Chapter 19

Riznar moaned staggering backwards, his vision blurring and eyes streaming bright, green tears. Lailoken screamed and smashed a fist onto the scrying table, sending a spider web fracture across the glowing green surface.

*

Moments earlier the pair had been engrossed; gloating over the fate of the escapees, as their troops encircled the them, deep in the Northern forest.

Then the horned one had intervened.

Even from the great height of the viewing table, the darkness of the forest was dispelled as the Lord Cerranos appeared.

"Gah! The tree God!" Lailoken hissed, spitting on the smooth surface, his spittle sizzling and smoking noisily, before finally frizzling away to nothing.

Riznar knew the tales of legend; Cerranos the horned god; keeper of the forest and glade; one of the elemental Gods created to care for the world.

"Divert half the troops from the riverside...kill them all," Lailoken ranted. "Do it now!"

Riznar scurried to the corner of the scrying table, where an assortment of bizarre implements were arrayed on the stone rim. He picked up a long, thin bone, and placed it to his full lips, whispering a silent incantation. Slowly the image on the table faded and swirled with boiling darkness, before reforming with the image of the River Ulfen.

Suddenly the swirling storm clouds of the tornado obscured the view of the tabletop. Lailoken gave another cry of frustration. The swirling vortex flashed and exploded soundlessly, as the view turned slowly green and a blob formed, blotting out the images on the table.

Slowly the entire surface began to glow, pulsing brightly. Riznar reached tentatively out with the sharpened bone, as the glassy surface began to bulge upwards, and a green sphere of luminescence floated free.

Riznar frowned as the ball, which seemed to contain a swirling mass of green worms, began to grow. It expanded slowly till it touched the outstretched bone.

"No!" Lailoken warned too late, stepping backwards swiftly.

The explosion threw Riznar back as he took the full force of the blast, splattering him with slime.

*

Riznar staggered around blindly, clawing desperately at his face, "Help me!" He reached out to his dark master.

Lailoken placed a bony hand on Riznar's forehead, and with a hard push, sent the fat man sprawling backwards. He cursed loudly, sweeping past the groaning Riznar, into a huge bay window. Growling a guttural command, he thrust his palm outwards, fingers spread wide. The glass shattered, sending the red velvet curtains flapping wildly in the swirling winds.

His face set in a snarl, as he shrugged off his robes, dropping the golden mask to the floor with a dull clatter. With a deep growl that ended in a high screech, he called out into the darkness, "**With talons sharp, and wings so strong, In the skies, I now belong**."

Thunder cracked nosily overhead and lightning lit the night sky, as Lailoken fell to his knees and raised his long thin arms. His legs shrivelled and shortened and thick brown feathers sprouted across his back. His nose and chin elongated, hooking and thickening into a sharp beak, and his arms broke and folded back, melting into feathery nubs that stretched and jointed into two broad wings.

The massive eagle leapt from the balcony, screeching into the night sky, high above the silent city. It wheeled several times flapping in long slow circles, gaining height before turning and soaring towards the distant river.

Chapter 20

Sigurd lowered each of his companions, one at a time, into the dark well. He secured the rope to the bars of the nearest cell and followed them into the gloom, his axe tied across his broad back.

Jack held his sword aloft. The fiery glow from the blade lit a large watery chamber of finished stone, half filled by a stream splashing noisily through from a narrow side tunnel.

"Hurry up, Sigurd! This water is f...freezing!" gasped Samanthiel, her breath fogging in the damp atmosphere, as the icy water lapped around her waist.

Sigurd slid quickly down the twitching rope and landed with a splash, sending a wave and a chorus of complaints and sharp intakes of breath, sweeping around the chamber.

"Must be this way." Jack ploughed through the water into the narrow passage, followed by Mistress Inga, her voluminous cloak floating around her like a black flower's petals.

Sigurd barely managed to pass, his shoulders scraping both walls. Samanthiel sloshed behind, glad to be out of the deeper well pool.

"All these years, I have lived here, and never knew of this place." Sigurd muttered, his voice almost drowned out by the rushing waters.

"These mountains are alive with water, Sigurd. This stream is but a diverted tributary of a larger river that flows beneath the land." Mistress Inga paused her dark eyes glittering in the gloom. "I can sense the tremendous energy close by."

As they moved deeper into the tunnel it widened and the water level gradually rose past their thighs, making every step against the swirling current a labour.

Suddenly the roof sloped down and disappeared into the rushing waters, Jack stopped abruptly and turned to his friends. "Dead end," he said simply.

Sigurd shook his head, heaving a deep sigh, "My Father's shade would...not...lie," He barged past Inga, pressing her against the slimy wall, forcing his way to the front.

"I didn't say he did, Sigurd." Jack began, before his massive friend took a deep breath and plunged into the water, and swam out of sight.

Samanthiel gave a small cry of alarm, but Inga merely stood silent. Jack turned pale, swallowing nervously. "If we follow, it will be in darkness..."

Sam smiled at his fear. "Don't worry Jack, I will pull you out if you drown!"

Jack gritted his teeth flushing with embarrassment, "I am not afraid!"

"I shall go next." Inga declared and she unwound her cloak and discarded the garment, letting the swift current take the black cloth back downstream. Her lean body was bound tightly with straps of dark cloth, covering her from knees to neck. She unwrapped a thin strip of cloth from her wrist and tied her wild hair into a ponytail, taking two or three deep breaths before plunging into the stream and vanishing.

Samanthiel began to unbuckle her leather armour, dropping each piece into the cold water. She soon stood in her white blouse and thin breeks, holding Nemesis's scabbard. It was her turn to flush as she noticed Jack's attention; her thin white top had become almost transparent in the cold, damp atmosphere.

Jack coughed and dropped the sword, instantly plunging the passage into claustrophobic inky darkness.

Jack felt a cold hand upon his cheek, and he jumped.

"I will be right behind you, Jack." Samanthiel whispered, her warm breath on his cold ear, sending a frisson of tingles down his spine.

Jack took several breaths, his heart racing, before plunging into the cold dark water. The pain almost made him gasp, the stunning cold seemed to press his head in its vice-like grip. He swept his cupped hands in swift, powerful thrusts, kicking furiously, with his eyes screwed tightly shut. Seconds passed, and the held breath began to burn in his lungs, as he fought the current.

Lights began to flash behind Jack's eyes as the current whooshed at him from a different direction, sweeping him in a tumble of froth. Panic swept through him and he began to exhale, kicking to the surface, knocking his head painfully on the jagged roof.

I'm drowning! Jack screamed in his mind.

A large hand grabbed his collar and hauled him upwards as the river opened into a huge cavern. Jack broke the surface spluttering and coughing water, arms and legs still thrashing wildly.

"Jack! You are through!" Sigurd shouted in the darkness.

"*Sword,*" Jack called groggily, holding his hand out of the water as his luminous weapon appeared, lighting the cave.

Samanthiel popped up next to him, her scabbard held between her clenched teeth. she exhaled with a soft hiss, hardly out of breath.

The four bobbed down the fast flowing river, the glow from Jack's sword barely lighting the nearest wall as they swept past. A deep rumble vibrated the air as the water seemed to speed up.

"Look ahead!" Jack cried, struggling to keep his sword out of the water.

A faint glow lit the next cave the river flowed through. Jack looked up to the roof and was both amazed and horrified to see a rope bridge high above spanning the cavern, joining two tunnels.

"Quick! To the wall!" Inga barked, swimming powerfully towards the cliff face. Sigurd helped Jack and Samanthiel, swimming easily despite the massive stone axe strapped across his back.

Jack gripped a jutting stone with all his strength, his fingers numb with the cold. The water seemed to suck at him ferociously almost willing him to let go.

Inga reached up for a handhold and pulled herself clear of the river, climbing nimbly up the cliff like a dark spider. Samanthiel followed, her sword once more between her teeth, her hissing breath was ragged and swift. Jack held on with his sword lighting the way for his friends, Inga made it to the safety of the bridge and disappeared into the mine tunnel.

She returned momentarily and dropped a rope over the side. Sigurd pulled himself up, puffing with exertion; the cold and climb taking its toll on the seemingly limitless energy of the giant man.

Jack grabbed the rope, plunging himself into darkness, the current swept him out into the middle of the river and he hung there twisting like a worm on a fishing line. He tried to pull himself up, but fatigue made his arms feel like rocks, and he sagged back into the river.

"Jack!" Samanthiel's cry of alarm echoed above as she hauled on the rope. Sigurd joined in, hoisting him clear of the rushing dark water.

Moments later Jack sat shivering on the thick wooden planks of the rope bridge, still clinging to the rope with clawed white hands. A single oil lantern hung from a post at one end of the bridge. The soft glow casting a yellow circle of light.

"I...I cant...let go of the...rope," Jack almost sobbed.

Inga pulled a small knife from the cloth binding her waist and made a small cut on the palm of her left hand. Dark blood welled in her cupped palm, she crouched down and breathed onto it, before reaching for a pinch of rock dust.

She stood straight and began to chant in a low throaty voice, mixing the dust and blood in her hand, till it formed a small dirty ball. Kneeling beside Jack, she blew on the ball and suddenly it exploded in a shower of small, bright sparks.

Jack was covered in the motes of light, and they continued to glow for a few seconds, flooding him with warm energy, before winking out. He lowered his head, a sad frown creasing his face.

"There is no shame in exhaustion, Jack." Sigurd placed a large hand on his damp shoulder.

"Are you going to sit there all day?" Samanthiel teased, fastening the buckle of her sword belt around her narrow waist.

Jack looked up at her and smiled. He rose shakily to his feet and took a deep breath.

"Thank you, Mistress Inga." He gave her a quick hug.

Inga took a step backwards frowning, unused to male contact. Sigurd laughed at her shock, and cast his gaze into the tunnel, "I have not been down here in the mines, but this way rises slightly." Lifting the lantern from the post, he headed off, up the slope.

*

An hour of winding tunnels, strewn with discarded mining tools, passed. More tunnels ran off from the main passage, sloping downwards, but the group continued onwards and upwards.

Sigurd held up a hand, halting them. "Shh! Listen…"

In the distance a roar echoed, it seemed like a crowd of cheering men, interspersed with an occasional ring of steel.

Sigurd's scarred face broke into a wide grin and he took off running. As they got closer, the noise became almost deafening, before falling silent for a few moments, then resuming louder than ever.

"What in the name of the Goddess have they got to cheer about!" Samanthiel cried.

She soon got her answer, for the passage ended in a huge room. A twisted wreck of metal framework and cages lay amidst a tangle of thick ropes. Men stood in groups, wide circles filling every spare space. In each circle two opponents faced each other with crude weapons drawn. The smell of unwashed flesh and the pungent tang of fresh blood was overpowering.

Samanthiel couldn't believe her eyes as she noticed a thin red rivulet running past her into the tunnel. Then she noticed the bodies; several dead warriors were laid near them, makeshift weapons still clenched in frozen fists of death.

Chapter 21

The last thing Belthor saw, as he tumbled through the air, was the smoking crater rushing to meet him. He tried to relax his muscles before landing heavily, slipping into a welcoming unconsciousness.

*

He became vaguely aware of several voices in the dim distance, then of being hoisted by his arms and dragged roughly down the steep slope, his legs raked by the coarse heather.

"Bloody weight!" one voice complained.

Belthor regained his senses, and feeling no broken bones or anything more serious than a burn or bruise, decided to play dead.

"This 'bloody weight' is Lord Belthor the Changeling, friend of Demons! Don't you remember the warnings the Lord Riznar gave?" another voice echoed.

"But...he cast a 'Four-Winds' spell," a younger voice started. "Surely if he was in league with the darkness, holy spells would be beyond him? I mean he actually used the names of power..."

Suddenly Belthor was dropped as one of the men carrying him seemed to lash out at the younger man.

"Are you in league with the darkness, apprentice?"

The cry of rage was followed swiftly by a vehement denial from the young man. A distant voice of command cried out. "Stop it, you two. Bring the Demon worshipper here, immediately!"

Four hands grabbed Belthor's arms and the downward dragging continued. He knew as the ground levelled out that he was headed towards the standing stone circle. The chink of metal rattled as he was slumped unceremoniously against one of the rough, granite obelisks. He let his head loll loosely against his chest as his arms were pinioned, fastened once again with manacles and chains, wrapped around the massive stone.

"I will place a mute spell on him, lest he wakens and tries to change into his...creature."

The commanding voice was close, it sounded like Lord Belkin: a very powerful and corrupt mage of the Magic Council. Belthor felt something being placed around his neck, followed by a strange feeling of tightness in his throat.

Mute spell indeed! He thought to himself.

Belthor knew that he did not need to speak the sacred Changeling chant to bring on his animal ways; a mere thought would suffice, but his enemies did not realise this.

"I must report to the Lord Riznar. I trust you will be able to control this prisoner until I return." Belkin's voice dwindled into the distance.

Belthor lifted his head till it touched the standing stone and slowly opened his eyes. Before him stood two red-cloaked men; one with a silver mask, the other, unmasked, the young apprentice.

"Kaleor! He's awake!" the apprentice yapped.

"I am not blind, Jared!" Kaleor gripped his silver tipped staff tighter. His mask bobbed nervously as he glanced from Belthor to his superior disappearing into the distance.

Belthor looked down at his chest, several strange items hung there, tied together by a small twine of human hair; a tiny dried tongue; a single tooth with dried blood on the roots; and two small slithers of flesh that could only be some unfortunate's lips.

He shook his head sadly, thinking to himself, *so they are using black magic now...these poor, misguided fools.*

Belthor fixed Jared with a steely stare, holding his eye for several moments before the apprentice flinched and averted his gaze. When the lad looked again Belthor tried smiling disarmingly. Amazingly, the apprentice gave a brief smile in return.

Suddenly Kaleor swung round and landed a hard punch on Jared's jaw, sending the young man sprawling to the ground, spitting blood.

Belthor growled menacingly, straining forwards till pain shot though the tendons and joints in his shoulders. He glanced anxiously left and right; seeking help. A little way off, the next group of chained victims stood together, watching the unfolding drama.

Kaelor swung his staff, cracking the young apprentice in the ribs. Jared let out a gasping howl of pain, sprawling to Belthor's feet. He looked deep into the old man's eyes, and made an instant decision. Before Kaelor could stop him, Jared reached up and swiped the black-magic items hanging around Belthor's neck.

"Break." Belthor spoke magically.

Behind the silver mask, Kaelor's eyes widened in horror, and he swung the staff at the captive. Belthor whipped his manacled wrist around and the loose chain shot out, wrapping around Kaelor's legs.

As the red, robed figure fell backwards, the young apprentice leapt upon him, striking the metal mask with a chunk of rock, making it ring with a dull clank.

Jared raised the stone to strike again, before Belthor intercepted him. "No, Jared. Don't kill him."

Kaelor lay unconscious, as Belthor rose, releasing his chains with a slight gesture. Jared stood wide-eyed, still straddling his fallen, former friend, the rock held loosely in his trembling hand.

Belthor reached out and placed a large, calming hand on the lad's shoulder.

"Thank you, Jared."

"Wh...what have I...done?" he stammered, a confused frown etching his purpled face.

"Jared, you have chosen your own fate, and chosen well, young man. There is a great evil being practiced here." Belthor paused, looking towards the huge cave that the monstrous creations had entered.

Jared followed his gaze and shuddered, "Great...evil?"

Belthor nodded, frowning grimly. "I was about to quiz you on the details, but it is apparent that your have been kept in the dark."

Belthor wobbled unsteadily between the tall stones, gripping the sharp surface as he staggered past. Jared leapt to his side, swiping Kaelor's staff, and offering it to the old man. Belthor shuddered, shrinking from the dark, polished wood.

"No, Jared. Can you not feel the darkness swirl within this staff? It has been tainted by the hand of a Demon."

Jared dropped the staff, "You mean Lord Lailoken. He is the Demon, isn't he?"

Belthor stiffened with more than physical pain, before nodding slowly. "Yes, Lailoken...is...possessed by a Demon."

Jared saw the emotion ravaging the old man's face, and he gripped Belthor's elbow, steadying him.

Belthor took a deep breath, still holding on to the stone, and studied the lad. Jared was slight, still sporting a full head of long, bright, red hair; apprentices didn't have their heads' shaved till they completed their training. His face was angular and despite the bruising, quite handsome, with high chiselled cheekbones and a small pointed nose, topped by a pair of intelligent blue eyes.

Suddenly Jared perked up, "Wait here, my Lord." he cried enthusiastically.

Belthor sighed, watching as the young apprentice sprinted off up the heathery slope and over the brow of the hill.

As the lad vanished, Belthor turned his attention to the chained captives; the forlorn and downtrodden people of Darkhaven; those unwilling, or unable, to fight.

Chapter 22

"Brothers!" Sigurd roared over the din of the fighting men. A spreading ripple of astonishment radiated outwards from the giant Grimswadian. Scores of shaggy heads turned, till every man faced the tunnel mouth. The nearest turned pale, wavering on unsteady legs, as the gathered men slowly fell silent.

The men made complex gestures, twisting their fingers into the sign of the horn; a superstitious warding intended to banish evil spirits. Mistress Inga pushed swiftly forwards into the room, dangerous fire flashing in her eyes.

"Kneel before your new Lord! This is Sigurd Grimsson, not some dark shade," she hissed.

As one, the men slowly lowered to one knee. The nearest man reached out, gripping Sigurd's hand, kissing his callused knuckles. Sigurd recognised Ragnar, his Father's weapon master.

"My Lord Grim! We thought you dead, Sigurd!" he cried, emotion thick on his gruff voice.

Sigurd pulled his hand away, wiping a tear from his eye. "I have not yet claimed my Father's crown, Ragnar."

Ragnar cast an uneasy glance at the bodies in the tunnel mouth, "Your Father...we could not," he faltered.

"Rise, my Brothers." Sigurd cut him off. "This is not the time for kneeling...this is the time for revenge!"

The sad shadow lifted from Ragnar's craggy face, replaced by the light of hope, and the burning desire for retribution.

Sigurd turned, ushering Jack and Samanthiel into the room. The men cast narrowed eyes over the young lad and the scantily clad girl.

Looking down at the blood slick floor, Samanthiel frowned. "Sigurd, why do these men of yours kill one another, whilst their enemy are almost close enough to smell?"

Jack looked up at the big man, who broke into a deep chortle.

"My Lady, my sword brothers cannot die of hunger or illness, or they will not enter the hall of heroes. They must perish in combat, and die with a weapon in their hand. Hence the fighting!"

"Brothers, these easterners saved my life, using feats of combat and magic that I never thought to witness in this lifetime. If we live through these coming hours, their names will be made myth and sung in every ale house from here to Haarsfalt!"

Jack swallowed hard, flushing slightly. Samanthiel smiled at the compliment, her face transforming beautifully.

*

Leaving Sigurd to make the introductions, Mistress Inga barged her way through the sweating throng of amazed warriors, heading to the twisted tangle of metal and rope.

The cage and lifting mechanism were smashed beyond repair. several men had been crushed by the falling wreckage, but the ropes seemed intact.

Casting her gaze skyward, she could see the stars far above; the assassins had set explosive charges in the wheelhouse and blown the roof clean off the building, sending the crushing wreckage down the shaft. The unconscious warriors would not have known their fate, and blessedly their end would have been instantaneous.

The huge shaft above was the only way out and she knew in her heart that climbing would be impossible. Inga wracked her brains, lost in thought; desperately trying to figure out an avenue of escape. Through her reverie she became aware of a figure to her side.

"Only one way out, eh?" Jack said.

"Yes."

Jack looked at the huge looping pile of thick ropes, each as thick as his arm. Samanthiel pushed her way though the warriors, "Come on then, Jack. Let's get out of here."

She nudged Jack with her elbow, giving him a secret smile.

Jack gave a small chuckle, "Sigurd," he shouted above the rumble of excited chatter. "Please ask your men to make space here. I don't want to hurt any of them."

One warrior, a giant of a man with a thick, bushy beard that reminded Jack of the Angel Zadkiel, started to laugh uproariously. He slapped his thigh and wiped a tear from his eye. "This whelp couldn't hurt a midge fly, Sigurd."

The men around him laughed a little and several stepped back nonetheless, as he unbuttoned his clothing.

Jack smiled at the overloud warrior, fixing him with a steely gaze. **"Dragon Fly... Dragon Eye... Dragon Be...DRAGON ME!"**

His voice deepened unnaturally, turning from a growl to a piercing scream. The circle of men widened quickly as Jack collapsed to the dusty, stone floor, twitching violently. His bones snapped loudly, jutting at painful angles as he writhed in agony. Jack's body expanded swiftly. Several men cried out in horror as he began to stretch and grow magically before their astonished eyes. Moments later Jack stood tall, resplendent in his green Dragon form. He had managed to remain conscious, the pain of the change becoming less of a shock to his young body.

Must be getting used to the pain, he thought to himself, proud of the fact.

The scornful warrior stood with his back pressed to the rough stone, mouth hanging open in disbelief as Jack's huge serpentine neck swung around and a large, smoky, yellow eye fixed him with a humour filled gaze.

"Watch I don't step on you, little man," his voice boomed telepathically around the room.

Samanthiel burst out laughing, patting Jack's sleek, scaly neck. "Well Dragon boy, what do you think?"

Jack lifted his snout to the shaft. "Sigurd, choose your six best men." He picked up two thick ropes with his powerful foot claws, flapping his wings slowly. He rose steadily coming to a hover with the ropes dangling.

"Cut the ropes!" he cried.

Inga whipped out her knife and began sawing.

Sam leapt to the fore, grabbing the thick rope, twisting her wrist around and gripping it tightly, snarling. "Six men, Indeed!"

She was followed closely by Sigurd and only four more burly warriors.

Jack took the strain, flapping harder, hoisting the six swiftly into the shaft. The walls sped past and the dangling warriors twirled and twisted, as Jack picked up speed.

They shot into the night sky, soaring on the cold wind. Jack dived towards the armoury, coming to a hover above the building as the ropes swung like pendulums. As they touched the ground, Samanthiel and the men dropped, slipping quickly into the building. Jack swooped back towards the mountain top and back down the shaft.

*

The alarm bells began to toll from the castle walls as Samanthiel strapped on padded leather training armour, fastening her sword belt at the waist. Sigurd hefted his huge axe, shunning the metal armour in favour of his bearskin cloak. Moments later another group of his warriors burst into the room.

Ragnar pulled two curved scimitars from the rack, whirling them in intricate patterns. "These'll do nicely."

Samanthiel peered out through the barred window. The walls surrounding the courtyard were lined with black-clad archers, bowstrings taut, drawing beads upon the doorway.

Sigurd picked up a targe, strapping the small, round shield to his forearm. He made ready to open the door, when Samanthiel placed a hand on his shoulder.

"Sigurd, wait...," she whispered.

Chapter 23

Lailoken plummeted through the darkness, furious rage clouding his thoughts. Ancient memories swirled in his mind; rancid remembrances of the trials and tribulations he had suffered at the hands of the Young Gods; his banishment to the Netherworld, the damnable prison realm; the eternal battle against the Angels and their master - Ulfner Darkbane; and more recently the loss of his demonic brethren to the circle of life.

Another of his adversaries had shown his hand, first the Rock Goddess had stolen their dark magic and now the accursed Green One had tried to blind him.

He swooped between the towering, moonlit clouds. The shining silver snake of the river Ulfen glowing far below, the dark shore mirroring the stars; with many thousand points of fiery red. With a flap of his huge wings he settled on the edge of the camp command circle; a ring of expensive tents housing the Lords and Ladies of Darkhaven.

Hunching forwards, he began to shed feathers, stretching and growing till moments later he stood a misshapen man once more.

A red robed sentry stood blinking behind his silver mask, eyes wide in terror. Lailoken's own dark eyes widened in anticipation as he raised a charred fist, bright dancing energy crackling between his bony fingertips. Before the guard could cry out, Lailoken pointed a thin finger at him and a ring of blue fire encircled his throat, stealing his voice. The doomed man staggered backwards, tripping over a tent guy-rope.

*

Lailoken paced through the circle of tents, pulling the still-smoking robe around his thin frame, adjusting the silver mask. He strode into the centre of the circle and raised an arm to the heavens, uttering a guttural cry. A bolt of lightning crashed from the boiling sky, striking a pile of chopped wood, setting it ablaze. Using a powerful voice, he spoke a compelling command that reflected from the clouds and echoed around the hills, "GATHER NOW!"

Dozens of Darkhaven's dishevelled nobles staggered from opened tent flaps, pulling on robes, askew masks hastily adjusted. They gathered in a grumbling throng, annoyed at their rude awakening.

Lailoken eyed the gathering with undisguised contempt. "Silence!"

"Send your half your army east. Destroy every living thing."

"East?" One Lord queried. "The Demon horde is in the west and..."

"Silence!" Lailoken roared again, "You will destroy everything: man, animal and tree, and if anyone..."

Suddenly Lord Belkin burst into the circle, "My Lord, we have..." He stopped mid-sentence, clutching at his throat with a strangled rasp, tearing his metal mask off.

Lailoken held a desiccated hand towards the newcomer, twisting it slowly into a crooked fist. Belkin turned a shade of purple and his eyes bulged in terror as he clawed ineffectually at his neck, before collapsing to the grass.

"Who else wants to interrupt or disobey my orders?" Lailoken slowly removed his mask, fixing the gathered gentry with a piercing gaze. A sharp intake of breath was clearly audible, but nobody uttered another word.

"Who orders this rabble?" Lailoken's lifeless eyes probed the crowd.

One man nodded to the prone figure curled on the ground. "Lord Belkin is...err, was in command, Lord Lailoken."

Lailoken gave an exasperated snarl. "Listen to me, all of you. You will go now, this very moment. Take up weapons and use magic to destroy. Destroy! Destroy!" Laioken's hypnotic gaze swept back and forth, captivating all the nobles till they joined in the chant.

"Destroy! Destroy! Destroy!"

Satisfied, he turned and left the tented circle, kicking the unfortunate Lord Belkin as he passed. He left the camp, heading north, towards the valley of the cave.

Chapter 24

Belthor studied the long line of captives snaking though the valley. They were chained together in groups of ten, blindfolded and manacled at the wrist and neck. Men and women of various ages cowered on the ground, raw and bleeding from the forced march, too exhausted and terrified to put up a fight.

Belthor's face twisted in disgust. Anger and bitter sadness combined to make him almost retch, tears blurring his vision.

Why? He contemplated the Demon's horrific actions silently for the thousandth time, shaking his head slowly.

Suddenly a deep rumble echoed from the dark cave mouth causing a ripple of fear from the captives. A cacophony of crashes continuously ringing through the entire valley, caused the ground to vibrate with each ringing blow.

Belthor stepped forwards, calling out in a reassuring tone, "Friends! Please don't panic."

He reached down and gripped the rusty chain collar of the nearest captive; a grime covered, middle-aged man, dressed in the once white tunic of a baker.

"Break," he intoned magically, and the brown metal disintegrated into small flakes, turning to dust. Belthor gently pulled the cloth blindfold and the man wept openly in relief.

"Thank you, thank you, my Lord," he blubbered in gratitude.

"Belthor, Johnnas the baker, call me Belthor."

"I found it!" a distant voice called.

Jared appeared over the ridge, waving something wildly over his head. He bounded down the slope, his red hair flying like a trail of flames behind him.

Belthor smiled as Jared skidded to a panting halt, presenting him with his surprisingly intact rowan staff.

As Belthor took hold of the staff, energy surged through his arm, his eyes flashed with a raw, molten power. "Release!"

A small sphere of light shot from the tip of the staff, and flew into the midst of the captives. The ball bounced back and forth, landing on the chains and blindfolds of each man and woman, breaking their bonds and setting them free.

The people rose on shaking legs. Some stood silently, whilst others wept or laughed uncontrollably.

"My friends, your ordeal is far from over." Belthor boomed over the noise of the sheer relief. All fell silent as he continued. "The despicable Demon that has wrecked your lives, is nearby. He has planned something terrible here, and I intend to try and find out what it is, and then try to stop him. You will need to gather your strength and go eastwards with this young apprentice..."

"Me?" Jared interrupted, incredulously.

Belthor looked at the nervous young man, "Yes, Jared. You must lead them, take the people deep into the woods. Seek Lord Alvor and the rest of the citizens of Darkhaven."

Johnnas spoke up, frantically, "I'll follow this here lad, he's a young wizard, eh? He can help us! Yes, if anyone can, a wizard can! Come on! Wot you lot waiting for?"

"Settle down, Johnnas. You will scare the others," said Jared showing a maturity beyond his years.

Belthor smiled and nodded, placing a hand on the lad's shoulder. "You will be fine, Jared. Please take care of these people. They have suffered terribly and are in great need guidance and wisdom."

"What are you going to do?" asked Jared.

Belthor turned to face the oppressive darkness of the cave and took a deep breath. "I am going in there."

Chapter 25

The muscles in Sigurd's shoulders tightened at Samanthiel's touch. A black fletched arrow thudded into the doorframe beside his face. Samanthiel dared a swift glance through the barred window, catching sight of dozens of black clad men, lining up in the courtyard, bristling with weaponry.

She ducked quickly back as an arrow shattered the thin glass, showering her with sharp shards. Drawing her sword, Nemesis, from its ornate scabbard, Samanthiel steeled herself, ready to leap into action.

Ragnar gave her weapon an appreciative glance, "Nice workmanship," he said, raising his bushy eyebrows.

"The best." She smiled at him from beneath her large round helmet.

"Can't be the best. The Grimswadian swordsmiths are unparalleled, best in the world," he replied with a broken-toothed grin.

Samanthiel laughed. "Ragnar, this is Nemesis, and he is not of this world, look!" She twisted the sword back and forth and the light reflected a rainbow hue in its shining depths.

Their banter was suddenly cut short when one of Sigurd's men gave a cry. "My Lord! They are wheeling out the cannons!"

Samanthiel chanced another quick glance; sure enough, the troops were positioning three large cannons, and readying canisters of charge.

Sigurd turned to face the group of warriors, speaking softly, "My friends, we must charge the cannons. It will be a noble death and a sure way to enter the Halls of Heroes."

Ragnar and the men silently nodded their commitment. Samanthiel drew a deep breath, knowing full well that the barbed arrows would punch easily though her padded armour. A deep calm filled her soul, as she sensed the spirit of her father watching over her.

I will be joining you soon, daddy, she thought to herself. In her mind's eye, she could almost imagine him smile and shake his head.

Sigurd placed a hand on the door handle, hefting his huge stone axe with the other.

Suddenly a piercing screech filled the night air, as a massive shadow swooped from the sky and a jet of liquid flame turned the battlements and most of the archers into staggering infernos.

Sigurd and Samanthiel leapt through the open door, followed closely by the rest of the warriors, charging headlong into the men loading the cannons, weapons whirling.

Samanthiel leapt high, somersaulting onto the barrel of a cannon. The startled assassins lunged at her legs, but she leapt over them and whirled, striking left and right into their undefended backs.

Sigurd roared with berserk rage. He cleaved and chopped, hacked and hewed, dealing death and destruction to anyone foolish enough to stand in his way.

Samanthiel danced among the black garbed men, crouching low and leaping high; her every move graceful and deadly.

*

Jack wheeled around and swooped once again, several arrows ricocheted harmlessly from his thick, segmented chest scales. He flashed along the battlements, his foot claws raising sparks, roaring and roasting, severing and snapping, driving the remaining archers from the walls. He landed on the battlements and surveyed the scene in the courtyard below;

Samanthiel and the men fought ferociously, holding their own against a highly skilled enemy of a far greater number.

Suddenly a high pitched wailing filled the night, drowning out the clamour of the battle. Dozens of Grimswadian women flooded into the fray, shrieking and wailing like banshees. Armed to the teeth, they wielded kitchen implements and wooden clubs of various sizes very effectively, and in a few brutal moments the enemy were overwhelmed, bloody revenge leaving every last one dead.

*

Sigurd continued roaring himself hoarse, cloaked in grief, swinging his axe left and right at imaginary enemies. Ragnar, blood streaming from several superficial wounds, tried to stop him.

"Sigurd!" he cried ineffectively, dodging the whirling red axe. "The battle is over!"

*

Jack leapt into flight, plucking Sigurd into the air with his foot claws. He carried the struggling man high into the air, circled the city several times before diving back into the castle courtyard, then gently lowered him to the ground.

Sigurd dropped his stone axe and started to fall, but was steadied as Samanthiel leapt to his side. She staggered under his weight, but braced him till his strength began to return.

Jack took to the wing again, climbing high in a wide spiral, before swooping back down into the mines to rescue Mistress Inga and the remaining warriors. Meanwhile Ragnar ordered the warriors to search the castle and the rest of the city, and drive out the remaining enemy.

Sigurd limped across the courtyard toward the castle gate. Samanthiel ran after him. "Sigurd, where are you going?"

"To retrieve my Father's head..." he said wearily. "There are funeral celebrations to arrange."

Chapter 26

Belthor took a deep breath, steeling himself, before striding purposefully into the gloom of the cave. The floor and walls were rough. Freshly hewn stone angled steeply downwards into the hillside, the roof supported regularly with massive tree trunk trusses and struts.

He gritted his teeth, softly touching the dead bark of the tree. *This is no natural cave... a tunnel more likely, but a tunnel to what?* he thought to himself as he paused to lift a lit oil lantern that was nailed to the tree.

He fastened the lantern to the end of his staff, and the lamp's light intensity increased dramatically, dispelling the gloom.

The booming concussions of sound echoed louder the deeper he travelled, each strike a physical blow that jarred every bone in his body. Gradually a putrid stench wafted from below, hot and horrible. A feeling of deep foreboding wormed its way into his stomach and squirmed there relentlessly.

As Belthor moved deeper down the tunnel, a low rasping moan could be heard between each ringing strike. He stopped short as a pair of glowing eyes appeared in the gloom below. Moving into the pool of his lantern light, the hideous Amalgam creature almost filled the tunnel. Twisted shadows of each face danced on the monstrous torso, seeming alive yet locked in terrible frozen torment.

Belthor's mouth formed a thin line, his eyes narrowing and his nose twitching unconsciously. He swung the lantern in a long slow circle, whispering urgently, then blew a pinch of rock dust into the air. A glittering wall of crystal light formed between him and the Amalgam creature.

Still it rumbled on, its huge hammers swinging pendulously. Belthor prayed, planting his feet in a wide stance, one hand gripping the staff, the other palm outward, bracing the wall.

The creature stopped before the wall of light, then swung the man-sized hammer. A mighty flash of light met the dark energy of the impact. A shower of hot sparks flew as the wall shuddered, and with the second blow it fractured, the light slowly fading, the wall dissolving.

Suddenly Belthor swung the tip of his staff into the face of the monster. The lantern shattered showering the beast with burning oil. It staggered back one pace, flames sweeping the upper torso and head.

Then Belthor whirled the staff above his head, before thrusting the tip of the wood deep into the red, glowing orb of an eye.

"Elohim!" Belthor cried the powerful word, channelling the power of the earth up through his feet and out the staff into the beast's head.

It gave a terrible roar of pain, as a flare of light burst from the eye. Belthor dug his heels in, tensing as his muscles twisted and writhed beneath his skin. The light crept inexorably all over the giant creature till, in a radiant, but soundless, explosion, it crumbled into a pile of individual people.

Belthor fell, panting, to his knees. The unfortunate victims lay dead in a smouldering mound, half blocking the tunnel. He reached out and took the outstretched hand of a young woman, closing his eyes and whispering a silent prayer to the Goddess. He felt her powerful presence fill him with vigour and warmth, driving away his deep sadness.

As he opened his eyes, the bodies flared in flames and reduced to a fine ash in moments.

"Thine is this kingdom, mighty Danu," he whispered in the darkness, moving through the settling powder.

The natural phosphorescence in the rock cast a faint light, and after his night vision settled he could see well enough to proceed. The booming ceased as Belthor moved deeper into the earth.

The passage widened and opened into a huge, dank and eerily silent natural cavern. A forest of stalactites and stalagmites hung from the roof and rose from the floor, forming massive columns. Piles of pulverised white rock indicated the path through the cathedral-like cave.

Belthor weaved his way between the broken stumps of rock, the path still sloping steeply into the bowels of the earth.

Suddenly a deep rumble shook the cave. Belthor could feel a dizzying rush of disorienting energy surrounding and swirling through him.

Must be close to the river, Belthor thought shaking his head. The natural power of the mighty river always gave off wild, disruptive, fluxional energy. He had never experienced a flux of this magnitude before though.

He gripped his staff tightly, swaying slightly, struggling to create a field of calm energy. Eventually he managed to dull the effect to a mild dizziness, before continuing.

Ahead in the gloom, a glow of deep, red light shone from what appeared to be a perfect stone corridor.

Belthor stopped at the edge of the smooth stone, his brow furrowing in confusion. The passage stretched off into a downward curve, large red stones glowing in niches in the seamless walls. He cast his mind back; searching to no avail, for any memory of a chamber beneath the River Ulfen.

Slowly he shook his head and sighed before stepping onto the polished floor. Suddenly echoes of ancient memories ebbed and swirled around him. Belthor stopped and closed his eyes; sensing the past: something older than time was buried down there, something that was meant to be left undisturbed.

Chapter 27

Sigurd stood tall in his purple cape of office, wearing only a simple band of gold around his forehead. His tied hair was plastered to his head by the teeming rain that fell from a dark sky. Weariness hung on his shoulders like a sodden cloak, while the rain washed away his tears.

At his side, Ragnar stood in silent contemplation, head bowed, with large drips falling from his crooked nose.

Mistress Inga, once again wrapped in a voluminous black cloak, approached with a line of similarly dressed members of her Sisterhood. Slowly, they surrounded the funeral pyre: a tall wooden platform, filled with kindling and dry heather. Sigurd's Father lay on the simple wooden structure; reunited with his head, his hands crossed over the hilt of the massive sword resting on his body.

Jack and Samanthiel, dressed once more in their own clothes, watched from a respectful distance as the people of Grimswade filed past the pyre, bidding farewell to their leader.

They had returned to Mistress Inga's home and retrieved their belongings and Jack now half sheltered under the bulk of his saddle.

As one, Mistress Inga and her sisters began to chant a low dirge, holding hands in a ring around the pyre. A thin line of white smoke rose slowly from the kindling, which rapidly burst into bright flames, lighting the darkness.

Jack stood, swaying wearily on his feet. It seemed like days since he had last slept. His breathing deepened, his awareness expanding as the bright flames enveloped the wooden frame. He began to sense bright beings swooping from the dark, pendulous clouds; the winged warrior maidens come to lead the dead heroes to their Hall. Streaks of intense soul-light shot skyward from the mineshaft and the crumbling pyre.

"It's over, Sam." Jack mumbled.

Her brow crinkled in confusion. "Over?"

"He has left. Lord Grim. He's off to the Hall of Heroes."

Samanthiel smiled wearily. "You are a strange one, Jack."

*

Sigurd ordered three days of feasting, to celebrate the memory of his Father; as was the Grimswadian custom.

Jack and Samanthiel turned down an invitation to stay and join the celebrations. Deciding instead to rest overnight with Mistress Inga, before continuing their quest for the book.

*

Mistress Inga stood by Jack's scaly snout, as he lowered his massive body to the ground. Samanthiel fastened the long saddle straps around his pale-green chest plate scales, before hooking her boot in the stirrup and hoisting herself into the saddle.

They overlooked the city from the hilltop, next to the ruined mine-works. The new morning brought clear skies and hazy sunshine. The panoramic view, of the city below and the deep forest with the high ridges sloping into the distance, was breathtaking.

"Go north, till you see a crescent lake." Mistress Inga advised. "I would progress on foot from there, as the ancient darkwood is so dense that light will barely penetrate the upper branches."

Jack lifted himself on powerful legs, stretching his tail and flexing his leathery wings. He swung his long neck round to Sigurd and Ragnar, who had taken time out from the celebrations, to see them off.

"Sigurd," Jack's voice echoed telepathically, "there is something I need to ask."

"Name it, Jack." Sigurd replied without hesitation.

"Will you send troops into the east and clear the mountains and roadways of Demons? The people of Ness need to restart trade with you and your merchants."

"It will be done, Jack. I will lead them myself. But you must promise to return here one day and choose a wife."

Samanthiel stifled a laugh.

"A wife!" Jack's tail whipped back and forth in alarm.

Sigurd nodded. "I owe you a blood debt. You and Lady Samanthiel will forge links of marriage with our people."

"That *will* be right." It was Samanthiel's turn to react with undisguised sarcasm.

Jack shook his large head, "You owe us only friendship, Sigurd. Besides, Mistress Inga has provided information that has saved us weeks of searching for Belthor's Sister. But we shall return, one day in happier times, this I swear."

Sigurd nodded, satisfied.

"You ready, Sam?" Jack asked.

She dug her boot heels into his flank, tensing, "Ready!"

Jack gave several flaps of his wings and took a deep breath, before soaring high over the castle and city below. He circled the hilltop several times climbing high on the morning thermals, till the small gathering of well-wishers were little more than specks. He wheeled around and turned his snout to the north.

"Don't go too high, Jack. It's bloody cold up here!" Samanthiel cried, the bitter wind bringing tears to her eyes.

Jack dived lower, gliding over the bobbled blanket of green spreading over the hills below.

As Grimswade dwindled into the distance, Jack's Dragon eyesight picked out the occasional flash of dappled light reflecting the sun between the trees ahead.

He turned slightly towards it, as Samanthiel cried, "Jack, I see the lake!"

"One step ahead of you, Sam."

Jack pulled a tight bank and dive, causing her to grip her pommel tightly and pull back on the harness straps. With several slowing back-flaps of his wings, as they circled, the water, now below.

Then Jack spotted a small pebble beach on the north bank of the lake, and moments later he pulled up and landed with noisy rush of scattered pebbles.

His stomach did a flip as he spotted something strange tied to a tree at the edge of the forest.

"What in the name of the Goddess is that?" Samanthiel cried, slipping Nemesis smoothly from the scabbard.

Chapter 28

Belthor knew in his heart that something dreadful awaited him at the end of the corridor, yet he continued on his spiralling descent, undaunted.

Each pace became a trial as the wild energy pulled him left and right, buffeting him back and forth as if he was caught in the grip of a hurricane.

The pounding began again, stronger than before, each blow sending concussive waves shooting up the passage. Belthor felt his small hairs rising, a feeling of oppressive doom grew as the spiral passage levelled off.

An inky square of darkness greeted him as he rounded the last bend. Belthor stopped before the black opening. He studied his haggard reflection in the glossy surface, before tentatively reaching out. His hand passed through the doorway, sending a ring-wave of ripples across the cold, liquid surface.

Suddenly a crackling surge of sparks spread up his arm. He barely managed to cry out before a gripping force pulled him through the entrance.

Belthor gasped with shock as the dark doorway deposited him, sprawling, onto a large square step. He rose slowly and peered over a high balcony, overlooking a wide cylindrical room.

Far below, three of the hammering Amalgam creatures stood around one of five remaining fiery obelisks. One stone lay shattered, pulverised into sharp shards. Belthor's stomach tightened as he half recognised the glowing symbols carved into the bright surfaces of the flaming rocks. They reminded him of the ancient words of power he had studied many decades before as a young apprentice, only sharper, more angular and runic.

In the centre of the burning circle of stones stood a massive, milky crystal cube, the air above it swirling with a colourful aurora of circulating energy. Every strike of the huge hammers sent sparks showering over the opaque surface, causing the colourful energies to dance and distort wildly.

Slowly Belthor edged from the top step unable to tear his gaze from the scene below. He tentatively stepped from the platform, moving down the wide stairway that curved down the wall.

A mighty seal, he thought desperately, *but sealing what?*

He gripped his rowan staff tightly and began to try drawing up earth power, as he picked up speed sweeping down the steep stairway. He reached the floor, swinging his staff and crying out, **"Ateh!"**

Nothing happened.

The three creatures ceased their pounding and turned in unison, glowing eyes fixing him with their horrible burning gaze. Panic squeezed his innards as he felt the acid of vomit rise into his throat.

Lumbering slowly, the gargantuan creatures began moving towards him. The rasping breath of the hulking creatures seemed muted as the dying echoes of the hammer blows were still ringing in his ears.

Belthor tried to still his wildly beating heart and felt for the currents of earth power flowing around him. Normally he would simply concentrate and the energy would flow like an eternal spring, but now it felt disjointed and warped, jagged and unruly.

Stilling his mind, Belthor used his second sight to see the swirls of the higher, astral energies, filling the room with a tornado of colours. Each of the remaining obelisks were beacons of fantastic light, conducting the power and weaving a mesh of binding energy around the pitch blackness swirling inside the crystal cube.

Suddenly Belthor realised a terrible truth: The stones were older than recorded history, an ancient version of the Mighty Seal, and the first stone - Ateh - was destroyed.

He adjusted his spiritual vision back to normal in time to dive away from the huge hammer that smashed the ground where he had stood a moment before.

Using his staff as a pole, he vaulted over the heads of the giants, sprinting to the Kingdom stone - Malkuth. He stopped before the rock, feeling the awesome energy and heat radiating from the carved surface.

Ignoring the searing flames, he placed a palm against the second stone and pointed at the monsters with his staff, crying. **"Malkuth."**

A pulse of intense heat swept through him blasting from the end of the staff, shattering two of the creatures with a powerful explosion of spiritual energy. The smoking bodies crumbled into ash, the bright souls of the captives swirled up through the dust, drawn swiftly into the colourful aurora above the cube.

Belthor cried out in agony and slumped to the ground, cradling his smouldering arm. He raised his head and was barely able to utter a swift prayer before the huge hammer hit, sending him flying across the room and crashing against the wall with a sickening thud.

Chapter 29

Lupin stood on a ledge in the foothills of the Giant's Teeth mountains, high above the roaring rapids of the river Ulfen. He stretched his shaggy neck and howled beseechingly at the moon. Moments earlier he had been surveying the distant opposite bank; when a sudden pain in his heart told him something was terribly wrong with his Father, Belthor.

He sat on his haunches and tried to relax, settling himself into a mystical trance. He opened his astral eyes and sang into the darkness between the stars. "White Brother! Hear my cry."

His hackles rose and hope blossomed in his heart as the swirling, colourful skies parted and a meteoric flash soared from the heavens.

Moments later a shimmering spectral outline of the white wolf stood before him; younger, healthier and free of all ills.

"Manwolf," he yapped happily, his bushy tail waving. "It warms my soul to see you!"

Lupin lowered his snout in deference, before meeting his sparkling gaze.

"Old friend, It is good to see you in fine fettle. The pack flourishes, and finally man and wolf live in harmony."

The white wolf leapt high, giving a joyous howl. Astral blue static discharged to the ground as his large pads touched the earth.

"It has been many moons since I have joined the Great Hunt. Why have you called me here this night, Manwolf. "

"My Father, Belthor, is in peril and I need to find him."

White wolf's tail curled over his back and he nodded eagerly, his tongue lolling, "The Bear's Brother! I know his scent well. It will be done, Manwolf."

Before Lupin could thank him, the white wolf leapt into the sky, trailing a luminous tail of sparkles, as he bounded from cloud to cloud, rocketing southwards across the river.

Lupin's heart raced with nervous energy as he leaped from the ledge, bounding swiftly down the rocky slopes towards the rest of the pack patrolling the river side.

A brown and white female, sniffed at him as he entered the pack. She gave a low whine. "You saw him, Manwolf. I can smell him," she yapped excitedly.

The pack gathered and Lupin gave a silencing bark, "Yes, I have spent time with the White One, and he is with the Celestial Pack helping us now."

The old leader had died in the monumental battle against the Demons, and his old pack now burst into a frenzy of yapping and howling happiness at the news.

"What is the word of the humans from the other packs?"

An older greying wolf pushed his snout through the pack of excited youngsters. "Manwolf, the humans are splitting into two large packs. One moving off into the treeless hills, and the other staying still, waiting."

Lupin absorbed the news.

What is Riznar playing at? he thought to himself.

"Thank you brothers and sisters, we need to remain watchful, for I fear the shadow of darkness rising in the east."

"We stopped them at the human city! With the Moon's blessing we will stop them once again, or join the White one on the Great Hunt." The old wolf growled with grizzly passion, setting the pack into a frenzy once more.

Chapter 30

Samanthiel stalked carefully through the long grass at the edge of the beach. Jack studied the strange thing in the shade; it appeared to be a small, bald, blindfolded child, slumped against the rope that bound it tightly to the tree. It's pale, green skin glistened with an almost luminous sheen.

As Samanthiel moved slowly into the shade of the tree, the round head whipped up, cocking left and right, listening with the long, pointed ears protruding above the blindfold. A strange gurgling whine issued from a small, wet mouth and a thin blue tongue flickered; almost tasting the air.

"Please," the soft, hissing voice pleaded in a hoarse whisper, "...no more. I have told you everything!"

Samanthiel stopped, sheathing Nemesis. Her brow creased and her mouth hung open in horror as the green creature began writhing against the tight rope, and small wounds crisscrossing the stomach and legs opened, oozing fresh blood.

"Be still, little one, be still." Samanthiel soothed.

"Mother?" It asked anxiously.

As Samanthiel knelt beside the tree, the breeze swished in the upper branches and dapples of sunlight washed over the captive. Instantly the skin changed from a smooth, iridescent, pale-green to a deep brown with rough scales sweeping over the affected areas. A piercing cry issued from the small being again and Samanthiel almost fell backwards in shock.

She stood, positioning herself so that the creature was cloaked in her shadow. As she reached out to loosen the ropes, Jack crouched low and whispered mentally to her. "Wait, Sam..."

He summoned energy and swiftly transformed back into his human form, retrieving clothes and dressing hurriedly.

"We are not here to hurt you." Jack spoke up, approaching from the beach, fastening his shirt.

The little head swept his way, flinching again and mewling with the pain. Samanthiel gently placed a reassuring hand on its thin bare shoulder and instantly it seemed to settle.

She drew Nemesis again, carefully slicing the ropes then untied the blindfold, sliding the rag up over the smooth head, and got a good look at the face of the unfortunate little creature. It sat there with eyes screwed tight, small ribs rising and falling rapidly as it almost hyperventilated.

"Do not look!" It cried in a high-pitched warning. "I am too weak...too weak."

Jack frowned at Samanthiel, who shrugged in similar confusion.

"We will not hurt you. I promise." Samanthiel soothed, giving Jack a little nod.

"Yes, you are safe. We mean you no harm," Jack added.

"No!" It sobbed, tears rolling from the tight eyes. "We are not safe! The shadow man is here in the forest and he is looking for Mother's book!"

Jack leapt to his feet, nudging Samanthiel aside, gripping the thin shoulders, "Did he smell of spice?" He demanded urgently.

"Yes, yes. Spice." It nodded.

Slowly the green eyelids slid open, revealing the most amazing eyes Jack had ever seen. Golden ringed green irises flashed on solid blue orbs with pinpricks of bright red pupils, but as they focussed on the kneeling lad, they began to change. The beautiful eyes turned smoky yellow with a pale-blue slitted pupil.

"Oh no! Not that! Please!" It wailed, the small body buckling and heaving under Jack's grip.

Jack gave a small shout of alarm and released it, jumping up in horror as the small body began snapping, twisting and elongating, with jutting bones growing and reforming in the all too familiar shape of a small green Dragon.

The tiny Dragon tried to move on wobbly legs, but collapsed into the grass, falling unconscious with a thud. Instantly it transformed back into the small green creature again and Jack began to reach for the discarded blindfold.

"Jack! What're you doing?" Samanthiel almost demanded.

"Protecting it!" he said simply.

"But...,"she began.

"Shh!" Jack whispered, crouching with a knee either side of the creature's head, tying the blindfold loosely. He placed a hand on either of the long pointed ears, closing his eyes and concentrating deeply. A soft glow formed around his fingertips, and slowly the wounds began to close and heal, till its breathing deepened. All of a sudden it began coughing, writhing on the grass in agony. It's breath becoming rapid and shallow, till finally it heaved a long shuddering sigh, then breathed no more.

Samanthiel's eyes moistened with tears. "Oh Jack." She whispered.

"No!" Jack shouted shaking his head and concentrating harder. The glow around his hands grew in intensity, and sweat sprang to his brow. Jack's hands began to vibrate and the cords of muscle in his arms tightened painfully. An involuntary groan escaped him and his lips drew back, baring his teeth, as the power grew.

Suddenly the bushes between the trees rustled, and a small red doe pranced nervously towards them, the liquid black of her eyes scanning the sad scene.

"Jack, look." Samanthiel whispered.

The deer moved cautiously through the foliage and stopped close to the small green creature, sniffing before lifting her head and staring deep into Jack's eyes.

"He is gone, young mage. Save your strength, my young one...is dead."

Chapter 31

Belthor's soul clung to life by a tenuous thread. He floated in the swirling ether above his battered and broken body. The astral shadow of the Amalgam creature looked, using burning eyes and limited intelligence, at the seemingly lifeless man. Satisfied, it turned and lumbered over to the second of the obelisks and commenced the smashing.

The broken staff was wedged under Belthor's body, and the residual power still flowed through the living wood into his spine. Bones slowly began to knit, and wounds to close. Belthor felt the inexorable pull of life as he merged swiftly back into his physical being.

The white-heat of pain washed away the tranquillity of the astral plane. The pounding of the twin hammers sent painful shockwaves reverberating through the chamber. He kept his eyes shut as the last of the life leeched from his staff, then the welcoming darkness of unconsciousness claimed him once more.

*

The hammering ceased but the vibrations continued for a few moments. Suddenly an icy cold, vice-like hand gripped Belthor's jaw tightly, twisting it back and forth roughly. "What have we here?" A deep voice echoed, a gurgling laugh was closely followed by, "How low the mighty Danu's servant has fallen."

The stench of charred flesh assaulted his nostrils and Belthor's eyes fluttered open. His stomach twisted as he recognised the dark phantom of Lailoken squatting on his haunches before him, the robe's crimson sleeve rolled back revealing the partially healed scorched flesh.

"Lailoken, my son, I know you can hear me in there. I beg your forgiveness." Belthor managed to gasp.

The Demon possessing his son curled back his lips in a terrible parody of a caring smile. "How touching...It is a pity he cannot accept your apology...in person. But soon you will be joining him..."

Lailoken burst into gales of horrendous laughter, giving Belthor's head a savage twist towards the centre of the room. The Amalgam creature stood with both hammers hanging near the strewn floor. Four of the six stones were now pulverised, the aurora above dimming to a faint glow. The cube now vibrated, pulsing with a dark luminosity. Pressing his dry lips to Belthor's ear, he whispered, "Behold... my mistress awaits you."

An unearthly moan sounded from the other side of the room, as suddenly the Amalgam creature swung his hammer at an invisible enemy.

The growing echo of distant howls reached Belthor's ear. The swirling lights atop the remaining stones flared brilliantly illuminating the spirit wolves that swirled and leapt all over the unnatural creature of darkness.

Lailoken roared in rage, dropping Belthor's jaw and leaping towards the tornado of light that now enveloped the monster. Lailoken summoned up a blast of energy, swinging the golden eagle staff at the swirling wall of astral wolves. Unfortunately for him the golden staff was met halfway by the blindly swung, man-sized hammer.

The explosion of dark energy scattered the wolves. It also destroyed the final Amalgam creature, sending Lailoken flying backwards, tossed like a dark leaf on the gale.

Belthor closed his eyes, imagining the weight of large paws on his shoulders, and a warm, wet tongue licking his face. A warmth spread from his shoulders, down through his spine, to circulate through his internal organs and bones. Muscles began to twitch and spasm painfully as his injured body regained strength and vitality.

A distant groan rang through the chamber. Belthor opened his eyes slowly and managed to push himself onto an elbow. He spied the body of his son, sprawled at awkward angles, twitching and jerking spasmodically. Slowly Lailoken rose like a ruined puppet; muscles working awkwardly on broken bones, and began moving towards the remaining stones.

Chapter 32

The small deer leapt into the bushes, and after a small pulse of soft green light, she emerged an old woman, decked in a dress of leaves. She was small and pale, with fine willowy features, and long, straight, silver hair hanging past her shoulders.

Jack sat among the twigs and leaves, still cradling the small creature's green head, weeping quietly. Samanthiel stood behind him, a hand resting on his shaking shoulder.

The old woman approached without a word, and stooped, scooping up the small body. Jack and Samanthiel watched as she turned and began walking slowly into the forest.

"Wait!" he cried, wiping his face and leaping to his feet. "I will carry him."

She shook her head, and spoke in a gentle voice, "No, Jack. He is my child. I will return him to the earth. But since the fates have driven you to this point, you had better follow me."

Jack nodded. "I am sorry."

She held out her thin fingers, whispering with a sound like the wind sighing through the trees. A soft glow formed in her hand and two long, green silk scarves formed magically.

"I would beg that you two wear these blindfolds. It will help protect my children against further harm."

"Are you...Gaia?" asked Samanthiel.

She looked at her and smiled briefly. "I have been called many names, my dear, and Gaia is one of them. I have felt the peril my young Brother faces, and the pain the Goddess suffers at the abomination's hand."

"Belthor!" Jack cried. "What has happened? Is he harmed? Where is he?" Jack blurted out the questions, till Gaia raised a thin hand, silencing him.

"My Brother is injured and in grave peril. He is somewhere long forgotten, deep in the earth. I cannot tell you exactly, but with the wild energy blocking my senses, he must be close to the River Ulfen."

"Wild energy?" Samanthiel queried, puzzled.

"It is said that before time began, the Goddess Danu and the Gods walked this earth. The Fallen One betrayed her, jealous of her beauty. She created the Demons in an attempt to destroy the Gods and their home. The Gods of nature banded together, dispensing mighty power to the Angels, and some of their human servants. They created a prison to house this fallen one, and the Netherworld to contain her monstrous children..."

"The Demon's Mother...," Samanthiel whispered her hand automatically reaching for her sword hilt.

Jack interrupted. "There is an assassin loose in this forest. His name is..."

"Garan Snare." Gaia finished for him, "I know of him and his troubled mind." Her face set firm, and a steely look entered her green eyes as she stared down at her child. "His time is short, he will soon drown in his own blood."

Jack was a little shocked by Gaia's vehement prediction, but tied his own blindfold nonetheless, Samanthiel reluctantly following suit, though she was not keen; knowing Snare was in the vicinity.

Gaia took Jack's hand, placing it on her shoulder. Samanthiel gripped Jack's other hand tightly and kept her other hand on her sword.

They began a long, winding march through the forest. Birdsong and strange cries echoed here and there, setting their nerves on edge. Occasionally a loud cry of sadness rang out, followed by Gaia's response in a strange language that neither Jack and Samanthiel had heard before.

After what seemed an age, Gaia halted, placing the dead creature on the ground, and told them to remove their blindfolds.

Lifting the cloth, Jack blinked in the shady green light. His blurred vision cleared, revealing a large clearing of compacted bare earth. Clusters of tiny mud built huts surrounded a main hall of interlinked branches, tied down from the still living trees, the foliage providing excellent shelter. A small fire burned in the middle of the clearing, over which a large, black cauldron bubbled noisily.

Something caught his eye and Jack whipped round, full circle, catching sight of furtive movement; small glances of green, the creatures darting from sight.

Quiet crying echoed between the trees, and slowly another, even smaller, creature approached, sliding a foot forward in small circles; feeling the way. It wore a loose blindfold, and Jack could see the shining tracks of tears on the smooth green cheeks below.

"Dada?" It whimpered.

Gaia wiped her tears, and led the small creature by the hand to the body of his Father. He reached down and ran a small trembling hand across the smooth head.

"Please...bring him back." It sobbed in a tiny voice.

Samanthiel broke down, the memory of her own Father still raw.

Jack's breathing raced, a tearing pain filling his heart with a terrible burning shame.

"I will." He whispered to himself. "I will...I will!"

Gaia reached out too late, trying to stop him as Jack threw himself onto the ground, beside the tiny child. He roared in grief, emotions running riot, feeling the Dragon spirit roiling within him.

"Danu, please help him! Ulfner Darkbane! Metatron! Michael! Gabriel! Sandalphon! Uriel! Raphael! Jophiel! Chamuel! Raziel!"

He clasped the small head and screwed his eyes tight in concentration and prayer.

Gaia gasped as a tiny ball of green light floated from the heavens, drifting lazily like a falling leaf, to settle on the ground beside the body. The air in the clearing stilled, the birds falling silent, bearing witness to the hallowed scene below.

The tiny green child pulled his blindfold off, unheeding of the danger, reaching for the ball. Samanthiel turned away closing her own eyes tightly, beading tears falling from her lashes.

The child picked up the small glowing ball staring with amazing eyes at the twinkling soul within. A smile lit the small face and it nodded, placing the small sphere on his Father's forehead.

The body gave a spasm, the legs and arms twitching and trembling violently. Then after a long hissing inhalation, he began to breathe normally.

Jack opened his eyes, looking down at the small child laying across his Father's chest, clinging tightly. He managed a weary smile, before rocking back on his heels, attempting to stand, but collapsing in utter exhaustion.

Chapter 33

Jared's lungs burned and the sweat running from his red hair stung his eyes. For several hours he had fled eastwards, leading the people of Darkhaven deep into the relative safety of the forest.

"Keep moving," he called urgently as the smell of burning wafted on the breeze, but the people had been force marched for days already, and hunger and exhaustion was taking a toll on the weaker survivors.

Fire, he thought desperately, *Oh Gods, it's a following wind, if the fire is large we will get overtaken soon.*

Jared was an apprentice in his eighth year of training, usually magical apprenticeships lasted twelve years, but he was a quick learner and had reached a competent level of skill.

He stopped, and instantly people sank gratefully to the ground. Jared looked upwards, seeing no gap in the leafy canopy. He climbed swiftly into the upper branches, till he could see the stars twinkling between the leaves. As he lay on the moss covered branch, he could feel the surging waves of energy flowing through the limb. He closed his eyes and concentrated on the forest, drawing power up from the earth, through the tree's roots. Using the upper branches to channel the power into the sky, he tried desperately to visualise rain clouds. The tree began to vibrate, showering the people below with leaves.

A fat raindrop splattered his cheek, followed closely by the noisy patter of rain on the surrounding leaves. Jared opened his eyes to see a mass of boiling clouds scudding in from the north, preceded by a strengthening chill wind.

As he reached the forest floor thunder cracked the sky and lightning flashed, then the heavens opened and a life-saving torrential downpour commenced.

Jared called everyone to their feet, and reluctantly the people did as they were bid.

"We have to move! The forest is ablaze and I have done everything in my power to stop it. Our fate is now in the hands of the Gods, but we must get moving now."

Suddenly the strengthening winds picked up further, developing into a severe storm. Trees swayed and bent against the weather, roots straining to hold them in place.

Jared gripped a branch and staggered, struggling to remain standing. A deafening peal of thunder sounded almost directly above them and lightning exploded the top of the tree that he had just climbed down from. A cascade of burning embers swirled on the gale like insane fireflies, and a branch fell to the ground, barely missing the young apprentice.

"Come on!" Jared cried above the tumult, reaching for the branch to use as a staff as another spear of lightning spiked the ground nearby.

The people did not need further encouragement, as they began to move quickly through the treacherous night.

Chapter 34

Jack sat up, his eyes bound by a cloth. He felt a presence at his side. A patter of small finger tips brushed him gently on the brow with a feathery touch, the sensation sending an electric tingle sweeping through his head and a burst of colours swirling in his mind's eye. Rejuvenating energy flooded through him, and all of Jack's muscles tightened then relaxed, leaving him fully refreshed.

"Thank you," a small voice whispered, then the presence faded and was gone.

Gaia's warm voice called out, "You may both remove the blindfolds. Gaath has gone now."

Jack lifted the cloth, revealing Samanthiel doing the same.

"In all my years, I have never seen anything quite like the spectacle you performed here today, young Changeling. I must thank you for saving Gaath. He always wanders too close to the forest's edge...," she spoke with a thick edge of emotion in her voice.

"I need Raziel's book, Gaia." Jack said simply.

Gaia shot him a mysterious look. "I do keep the book, but will you be able to see it?"

Jack looked at Samanthiel, who shrugged.

"I don't understand," he said.

"You will, Jack, you will. Follow me, both of you."

Gaia turned and glided gracefully out into the clearing with Jack at her side. Samanthiel followed, eyes down, painfully conscious of the creatures watching from the shadows, but determined not to look.

At the far side of the village a well worn path led between towering trees into even denser woodland. Gaia stopped them before they moved into the shadowy gloom. "We are about to enter a very sacred place. I would ask that you please leave your weaponry here."

"I, for one, would prefer not to." Samanthiel stated.

Jack gave Samanthiel a reassuring nod. The flint hard gaze from Gaia, made her uneasy and she swiftly unbuckled her belt and hung her sword from a low branch.

Gaia vanished into the gloom, and the pair scrambled to keep up. The air was warm and choking in the absolute stillness of the shadow. Samanthiel's breathing quickened as the darkness enfolded them and suddenly she became acutely aware of her heartbeat thudding noisily.

Sensing her discomfort, Jack reached out and took her hand giving it a reassuring squeeze and she smiled, glad of the contact.

Gaia led them onwards up a steep track between towering trunks adorned with crude twisted grass figures, and twigs tied in strange bundles. As they passed the symbolic totems, a tingle ran up Jack's spine, and the small hairs on his forearms rose in a wave of goosebumps.

Jack's breathing became laboured and sweat dampened his shirt as he struggled to keep up with the small woman, who, despite her obvious age, seemed to possess boundless energy.

Finally two massive trees leant together forming a living arch, through which they could make out the outline of a dark doorway.

Jack strained, trying to discern the shape of the building ahead. It seemed to him that the frame and lintel were built into the side of the hill.

"Gods and Angels once walked this earth," Gaia began in a hushed tone. "Their servants, mankind, built them a fantastic city, and in ages long past this very location housed the 'Temple of the Creator'; a place of mystical wonder. It is written that the Gods grew powerful and corrupt, squandering the energy given freely by the Creator. They fought amongst themselves other over petty issues, and eventually a delegate of priests and mages petitioned the Angel Raziel to gather the knowledge of the Gods, and in doing so discover a way to separate and isolate the warring deities. Gods, Angels and men came here to worship, and the learned Angel Raziel complied his book of their... mysteries. He studied each and every deity, quizzing them on their powers and jotted down everything in one tome of the utmost import."

"Doesn't look much like a temple." Jack said.

She laughed and a twinkle entered her eye, reminding Jack of his Grandfather, Belthor.

"It was a temple, but nature has crept and covered, holding and hiding the secrets that lay beneath this magical forest. It has permeated everything, including my children, those the brutish Grimswadians ignorantly call ghosts..."

Jack closed his eyes trying to imagine the city and temple buried beneath the trees.

"This hill..."

"Yes it is, Jack." Gaia answered his unasked question.

"Is what?" asked Samanthiel, puzzled.

Jack smirked, "This whole hill is the temple, and that arch is the entrance."

Gaia nodded. "You are almost half way up a massive pyramid. Raziel's chamber," she raised a thin arm, "is right over there."

Samanthiel's mouth hung open in amazement, she had never imagined anything bigger than her bridge-city home of Ulfenspan,

"Come on Jack, let's go and get this book!" she cried enthusiastically.

Gaia led them through the white stone entrance, into a short passage of well swept marble. The air was cool and welcoming, fragranced lightly with hanging herbs and garlands of dried flowers. Bright shafts of sunlight filtered down from crystal panels built into the roof of the tunnel, and Jack marvelled at their flawless construction.

The passage opened into a wide glowing room, a beam of pure white light shone from a suspended prism, casting a rainbow light all round the hall.

Jack craned his neck studying the room; the entire roof was intricately carved with the sun, moon and stars, and a dozen doorways exited the room; four on each wall.

He was about to ask a question, when Gaia answered his query again.

"The apex of the temple is far above the forest, and a capstone of the purest crystal channels the light throughout the whole temple. The light has a calming effect on the soul."

Gaia walked to the centre of the room, where a small plinth rose slowly with a hiss. The black veined marble was embossed with a dozen ancient symbols and glyphs set in a circle. As her thin fingers danced over the markings, the huge prism began to rotate slowly, sending a cascade of colour swirling everywhere.

A low vibrating hum built and Samanthiel shielded her eyes as the light intensified, the speed of the crystal increasing with each moment. Radial spokes of light suddenly lanced outwards from the plinth, illuminating the doorways, each a glowing spectrum of brilliance.

Jack felt like a child seeing his first rainbow, his jaw hanging open in awe.

"Come, Changeling. We have destiny to fulfil." Gaia said moving towards the largest of the bright doorways.

Chapter 35

Growing wild energy flared brightly around the room, arcing from the jagged tops of the shattered stumps to illuminate the cube, before frizzling into the fading aurora above.

Belthor watched helplessly as Lailoken hobbled on crooked legs, stopping between the two remaining magical stones, blackened arms outstretched.

The crackling power surged again. A spear of energy shot from the stone, lancing through Lailoken, into the cube, forming a continuous flow. The square crystal began pulsing, revealing a swirling darkness curled within.

A single tear of frustration ran down Belthor's cheek as he gasped through gritted teeth, "Danu! Give me strength!"

He struggled to his knees, ignoring the breathless pain of broken ribs. Grasping the longer piece of the rowan staff, he jammed it into the ground, pushing himself shakily to his feet. Sweat dripped from his the tip of his nose as he shuffled slowly across the rubble strewn floor, every step an effort.

Belthor squinted against the intense light that surrounded his son. Lailoken had become an indistinct silhouette between the stones, arms flung wide and head back.

Belthor knew enough about wild energy to know that he should not get too close for the enormous potential energy generated by the millions of tonnes of water roaring overhead was unpredictable; held in check and harnessed by the standing stones since time immemorial. Now it was almost free.

In a desperate gesture he launched the broken staff, javelin style, before collapsing, face first, into the sharp rubble beside the glowing cube.

The wood clattered off the top of the crystal cube, and struck Lailoken under his chin, sending him collapsing backwards. Unluckily, the staff rebounded, wedging between the crystal and the last standing stone. The roaring energy surged through the staff and the crystal glowed brighter still.

Belthor raised his arm, shielding his face from the intense radiant heat. He had to scramble and pull his way backwards, sheltering behind the stump of a fallen stone; for slowly, in an incandescent trickle, the crystal began to melt.

A deep chuckle echoed around the circular room, as Lailoken appeared beside him.

"You have my thanks, Belthor. You have saved this frail body ages of pain. Truth be told, I doubt I could have survived it, nor would your precious son. But it is the price I would gladly have paid to free my Mistress."

Sour anger hardened Belthor's resolve, the beast had his son, and he would make it pay for that mistake.

It's better for him to die, Belthor thought grimly, *than exist in hellish torment.*

He lifted a hand towards the still-smoking Lailoken, his red robes singed and sooty. Lailoken laughed, suspecting Belthor was reaching for his Son's help in a pathetic gesture.

Instead Belthor was tapping into the abundant power circulating around the room, as he formed a ball of energy and with a strong thrust of willpower, threw it into Lailoken's chest.

The small explosion hurled Lailoken backwards, his robes flapping like dirty wings and catching fire. Rage lent Belthor strength, and he rose like an avenging angel from the rubble, his robes floating behind him caught in the circulating vortex of air drawn to the melting cube behind him.

Lailoken lay against the wall, the flesh of his chest and abdomen bubbling as the ring of flames finally died. He opened his eyes as Belthor's shadow fell over him.

"Does it not pain you to see your Son injured like this, Belthor?"

Belthor stooped and picked up a sizable chunk of rock from the floor, then slowly raised his hand.

"Demon, you will now join your hellish brethren in the afterlife, where my Goddess Danu will send you on to the Creator herself to receive your final judgement."

Laioken's eyes flickered to the cube and the flaking skin of his face cracked as his smile widened. He began to laugh horribly.

Belthor raised the heavy stone, ready to strike, when he felt the hot prickle of a presence behind him.

"STOP" the compelling command rooted him to the spot magically.

Chapter 36

Jack stood before the glowing doorway, Samanthiel at his right shoulder and Gaia, silent, at the other.

She expects me to know what to do, he thought carefully, *here goes.*

Jack closed his eyes and the darkness turned red through his closed eyelids. He relaxed feeling the warmth of the light bathing his face. A strange feeling of well-being filled him, and he became acutely aware of the sheer power thrumming inches from his face.

He began to feel with his mind, and instantly was hit by the strongest feeling of déjà vu. Instinctively he raised his arm and drew power though the palm of his right hand, creating a ball of light.

Samanthiel watched as Jack stood motionless at the bright doorway. She jumped when he suddenly broke the silence, speaking in a voice that seemed too deep for his young throat.

"Open."

The bright opening faded, turning black. Samanthiel blinked; the retinal flare sending colourful blotches floating in her mind's eye, making it hard to see that the doorway was now an opening, leading into a darkened room.

She looked at Jack standing there with his eyes still closed. She was slowly learning not to be surprised by Jack, and his amazing abilities. Then she glanced at Gaia, who smiled and nodded with a look of mysterious contentment.

They stepped across the threshold into a simple square room, illuminated by a single shaft of pure light in the centre, shining down on a stone table. A large, leather bound book lay open on the surface. As they approached the table, Jack shuddered as a wave of prickles washed over his face. The book, although still, appeared to vibrate. Jack closed his eyes briefly and shook his head, and when he reopened them the shimmering continued.

Samanthiel leant closer to the table and static crackled as her white shirt pulled towards the book, causing her to jumped back in alarm.

"It 's blank!" Samanthiel cried.

"Is it?" Gaia asked, feigning surprise.

Jack confirmed Samanthiel's statement; the page was indeed a plain, creamy vellum.

This can't be right, he thought saying nothing.

Gaia waited patiently, a slight smile playing across her face.

"When Raziel made this book...," Jack began, "he would not want just anyone to be able to read it..."

Gaia nodded, her encouraging smile widening as realisation dawned on Jack's face. He slowly lowered himself into a sitting position; legs crossed beneath him. Settling into himself, he began to feel for the energy, circulating it around himself in a continuous loop. Excitement grew within him, and his breathing quickened. He deliberately settled, damping down his emotions. Then he willed himself to rise.

Samanthiel looked at Jack sitting with eyes closed, first smiling, then frowning, before finally his features went slack; as if he slept. Her own breathing quickened and heart raced with barely suppressed excitement. Gaia moved behind Jack and rested a long fingered hand on his shoulder.

Jack's spirit stood beside the table, the silver cord of consciousness linking to his physical self. He looked at Gaia standing behind his body, surrounded by the fierce white glow of her aura. He was aware of her light touch on his shoulders;

more than a steadying presence, he was sure she bolstered his energy too.

The book was perfectly still on the table, although now the pages glowed with a golden light. Jack moved closer and he felt the draw of power radiating from the flaming words that danced on the page. As his hand touched the page, a deep, warm voice entered his head: "Heed these my words: Knowledge is power."

Jack nodded, answering, "Knowledge is power."

The voice answered with finality, "So...be...it."

Before he could react, the pages flipped in a blur and the bright words faded from the book. The flaming letters crept up his arm before vanishing into his soul. The ancient lore of the Gods; their long hidden secrets burned deep into Jack's mind.

Jack floated backward, his stunned mind reeling. Behind him, Gaia gave a small cry and quickly removed her hand from his shoulder; as if it was hot. She quietly hoped that Jack would be able to cope with the newfound knowledge.

Knowledge is power, Jack thought repeatedly, teetering on the brink of insanity, as the echoes of magic sank safely into his subconscious. He stood motionless till the buzzing subsided.

Jack was about to will himself back into his seated body, when he noticed a dark form slipping into the room. The entity flowed through the ether and settled behind Samanthiel. A feeling of dread swept through Jack's soul. With a thought he popped back into himself, swivelling in time to see Samanthiel's mouth open, a look of surprise on her face.

She gave a small step forwards, a blossom of red staining the front of her shirt. Jack watched helplessly as the stiletto point of a blade burst through her shirt and the dark hooded figure of Garan Snare, materialised at her shoulder.

He pushed Samanthiel forwards, twisting and pulling free his killing blade. She fell to her knees before Jack, her mouth opening and closing ineffectually, a thin trail of bright blood trickling from the corner of her mouth.

"This book is mine..." Snare said with a snarl.

"Sam!" Jack screamed as Samanthiel slumped face first onto the floor, a dark circle spreading beneath her.

Snare lifted the book, his brow creasing in confusion as he realised the pages were blank.

"Spear!" Jack cried. The long fiery lance appeared in his hand, and he thrust it with all his might at Snare's throat. The flaming weapon hit its mark, piercing the assassin's neck in a spray of blood. The mighty thrust propelled the assassin back into the wall of the temple, the raw wound sizzling around the living flame.

Snare's eyes bulged in horror as he was pinned to the wall. He scrabbled frantically for the magical ruby hanging around his neck, but no sound issued from his torn throat. Bloody froth bubbled at his lips as he slowly drowned in his own blood, just as Gaia had predicted.

Jack left the assassin to die, dropping to his knees beside Samanthiel. Breathlessly he rolled her over onto her back, the soaked shirt staining his hands. He stared at his crimson palms distractedly, his sobs coming in deep shudders.

"She has gone, Jack." Gaia said quietly.

"What? She is still here...gone where? She can't be gone...look at her!" Jack babbled.

A sharp, stinging slap cracked across his face. Gaia towered over him, rubbing her sore hand.

"Samanthiel is dead, Jack."

"No..." Jack said.

Jack raised his head and fixed Gaia with a hard penetrating stare, his eyes flashing golden for a moment. "Things have changed remember, Knowledge is Power."

Chapter 37

Raw fear and deep dread swept through Belthor as the powerful female voice echoed magically through the chamber. He stood rigid, the weighty rock above locked into position, unwavering. Whatever was encased in the crystal was now standing behind him.

Beneath him Lailoken licked the blood from his lips, eyes wide in anticipation.

"Meet my saviour, the dark Angel, Lillith the fallen, unbound, finally freed from her unjust holding," Lailoken cried above the crashing tumult.

"Cease!" Another word of great magic diverted the wild warping energy and the chamber fell into echoic silence.

Belthor felt, rather than saw, a flowing movement behind him; catching a glimpse of a glowing figure. Suddenly searing pain shot through his face as bright fingers caressed his chin momentarily.

"Lower your weapon, Bethor the Bear." A female voice whispered in his ear, her burning breath cold as ice.

Belthor tried to resist; a futile gesture. He lowered the stone against his will, dropping it noisily on the floor by his foot. He winced as the nude, winged figure moved fully into view. She was painfully beautiful; her luminous face, flawless and noble, was framed by black hair that hung long and straight, shining like melted tar. Her skin glowed with an inner fire that was brighter than the full moon.

Belthor's eyes glazed over, and a single tear ran from his eye as he swam in the pure darkness that floated in her over-large, pitch-black eyes and in the lost moments he forgot himself; forgot his family; forgot even his Goddess.

Lillith gave a small dismissive gesture with her finger tip and Belthor stepped swiftly aside his face a mask of mindless adoration. Her slender arm reached out and offered a delicate hand to the slumped figure.

"Rise, faithful servant." Her voice husky.

Lailoken rose, transforming. His wounds closed and healed swiftly. Long wasted muscles thickened and grew strong. Even his charred skin regenerated under the sizzling touch of Lillith, his dark Angel, but all of her healing could not return life to his soulless eyes. She gently ran a crackling finger tip along Lailoken's jaw line, her touch left a faint web of frost on his cheek, "Together we will leave this place and complete the work I began so long, long ago."

Lailoken gave a shiver of pleasure as his skin blistered painfully before healing. His eyes narrowing as he cast his gaze at Belthor, "What of this servant of Danu? Shall I tear him to pieces for you, my queen?"

Lillith turned to Belthor, her dark eyes widening in pleasant surprise as if seeing him for the first time, she leaned close and sniffed.

"Yes...I smell her taint upon this mortal."

She paused, considering. Then gave a small chuckle, "Yes...I shall make a plaything of his immortal soul."

Chapter 38

Lupin raced southwest across the grasslands at the head of the wolf pack. The information from the white wolf had turned his world upside down; his possessed brother Lailoken had taken Belthor captive in some secret chamber far below the river Ulfen.

*

Lord Ness sat alone in his private room. Life had begun returning to normal, with the arrival of the farming folk from the high pastures. Civil unrest faded and the curfew that they had needed to impose was finally lifted.

The weight of losing his friend Belthor had hit him hard, and he felt partially responsible, though in truth, the best security in the world could not have prevented his abduction.

Lupin had arrived earlier and they had discussed the White wolf's findings. Ness had no idea what lurked in the secret cavern, but he knew a man who might.

A simple stone bowl and jug sat on the table before him. He reached out and filled the bowl to the brim, and settled his hands flat on the table on either side. He closed his pale blue eyes, stilling his mind and drawing his attention into a sharp focus level, concentrating deeply on his friend, Belthor.

Slowly he opened his eyes, casting his sight and intent into the shadowy depths of the reflecting water. Vague shapes and colours swirled into view, but the fleeting images were swept away quickly.

The damned river is blocking my view, he cursed to himself. He sat for a while thinking, then decided to try another avenue. He tried picturing his old friend and tutor, Master Alvor. The water began to change colour; the dark shadow glowing with a green tinge.

The old mage's face swam into view, he looked exhausted and filthy, but was smiling a toothless grin nonetheless, talking animatedly to several men, before noticing the glowing communication orb floating nearby.

"Ness? By the Gods! You have a strong link here, well done, lad, well done!" Alvor cried in delighted amazement.

Despite the seriousness of the situation, Ness smiled; pleased that his old teacher remembered him after more years than he really cared to recall.

"Master Alvor, we need your help." Ness began. "Belthor is lost, his son Lupin reports that he is incarcerated in a deep chamber, far below the mighty river Ulfen."

Alvor's heavy lidded eyes narrowed and his bushy, white eyebrows dipped into a deep frown. "Below the river you say?"

He turned his back on the orb and faced the gathered men, conferring quickly. Ness sighed with frustration as the sound faded from his ears, but he watched intently as Alvor gesticulated wildly.

After a few moments and several solemn nods from the gathered men, Alvor faced him yet again, the sound returning.

"Ness, the chamber below the river is not mentioned in any schooling, but the ancient knowledge is passed down from master to master through out the years."

He took a deep breath before continuing, "It is said in ancient lore that there was once an Angel named Lillith. She challenged the pantheon; created the Demons: and tried to overthrow the work of the creator herself! The Gods united and imprisoned her deep in the earth, sealing her within a crystal prison for all eternity."

"The Demon plans to release her, that much is obvious. Once she is free, what will she do?" Ness asked.

"Once she is released, she will finish the work she started aeons ago. She will be free to wreak her revenge on us all, the children of the Gods..." Alvor said sadly.

Chapter 39

Jack knelt in the sticky pool, the warm air cloying with the scent of death. He closed his eyes, desperately searching for a healing spell. Deep in his subconscious something green and growing crept forth, twisting and turning like a snake. The healing power of nature writhed and boiled within him.

Gaia gasped, stepping back as the floor cracked and began to rise in a lump, splitting in a circle around the pair, green shoots sprouting. The tendrils threaded and wove into a grassy mesh that enclosed Jack and Samanthiel. It glowed with a pale green light, before fading and vanishing in moments.

Jack opened his eyes slowly, then reached out with trembling hands, pulling open a few buttons on Samanthiel's shirt. The wound that had pierced her breast had healed, leaving her perfect skin flawless.

"Her body is whole, but her soul has flown, Jack." Gaia said quietly.

On the wall, Snare had finished twitching and the spear dissolved, letting the assassin slump, lifeless, into a sitting position.

Jack shot him a narrow-eyed glance. "I managed to bring back Gaath's soul. I must try, Gaia!"

Jack sent out a cry to the Goddess Danu and the Angels, as he had done before, concentrating all his will, shaking with desperation.

Suddenly a large ring of bright light materialised over Samanthiel's body. Jack gave a shout of surprise when an Angelic face appeared within the circle; it was the Raziel: the Angel of Secret Knowledge.

"Jack, the Lady Samanthiel is trapped in an afterlife of her own creation. She was troubled in life, and this has passed along with her, through the shock of her untimely demise." Raziel's mellow voice drifted from the astral plane.

"I can help her." Jack said with simple conviction.

Raziel smiled, "Yes, Jack. You can, though it is perilous for both of you. For if you fall here, in the Astral, you will not be able to return."

Undaunted, Jack cried out. "What must I do?"

The glowing circle faded as Raziel whispered, "Knowledge is power, my young friend."

Gaia stood a silent sentry as Jack settled and closed his eyes yet again, pulling down energy into his body. Moments later he floated clear of his body. The room swirled with the dark colours of death and anger, red clouds of rage swirled and twisted like winged serpents. Gaia shone like a beacon in the haze, pure and bright, surrounded by the light of love.

She looked up at Jack's hovering soul, "May Danu guide and keep you safe, Jack."

What now? he thought to himself. Then Belthor's teachings came flooding back, remembering the last lesson he had, before Garan Snare had turned his world upside down.

Thought...Thought is the key! I just need to think of her, and I will go to wherever she is trapped.

Jack willed himself towards Samanthiel, and suddenly a golden doorway appeared in midair before him. Slowly he began to approach the threshold.

A huge, booming voice halted him halfway through.

"I am the Watcher at the Threshold, and none but the dead may pass me into the afterlife."

Jack could see nothing but the void ahead, but felt a tremendously strong being holding him in check.

"I will cross this threshold, and will return with my friend Samanthiel."

"Do you do this for love?"

Jack was caught off guard by the question, and even more surprised by his automatic answer, "Yes."

"You must be willing to share of yourself with Samanthiel. All you possess, for the remainder of your allotted lifetime, shall be divided unto her. Are you so willing?"

Jack was thrown again, *share everthing?*

"Yes...yes I am willing."

"So...Be...It."

Free once more, Jack passed into the void. The bright doorway winked out, leaving him in utter darkness. Thinking once more of Samanthiel, sent him hurtling through the nothingness.

Soon a pin prick of light appeared in the distance, growing rapidly into another doorway, which sucked him through and ejected him into Samanthiel's afterlife.

*

Samanthiel heard the screams, and lifted the hem of her gown, rushing towards her Father's tower. She pushed her way along the bridge town street, against the steady flow of people, streaming away from the tall towergate.

The sound of battle echoed from the tower, and she grabbed hold of a soldier who was running with the civilians. The man was bleeding from a gash on his forehead and his eyes were wide and wild.

"What's going on down there?" She demanded savagely, shaking him to his senses, splattering herself with spots of his blood.

"Run! Run, there's a bloody Demon in the first tower! It's unstoppable!"

He lashed out, knocking Samanthiel backwards, but she managed to grab hold of the crossbow that was strapped to his back as he fled into the crowd.

She pulled one of the six bolts that were clipped to the stock, and loaded the weapon. The rush of people fleeing the tower dwindled, and moments later the street was empty. Complete silence greeted her as she stepped into the tower entrance.

The carnage was complete; bodies lay everywhere, blood pooling and trickling; the stench of death was overpowering.

Samanthiel's heart beat wildly as she sprinted along the corridor to the high balcony overlooking the hall entrance at ground level below.

Her father stood among the bodies, swords crossed with another soldier. They faced off, and Samanthiel stood transfixed as the soldier he was facing, laughed horribly, the sound echoing around the empty tower.

"Daddy!" she cried.

The possessed soldier's head whipped up, locking eyes with Samanthiel, eyes widening in anticipation. Her Father took the advantage, delivering a deadly slicing blow to the head.

The soldier sprawled backwards in a spray of blood, crumpling to the floor. The body twitched for a moment, before a small black sphere rose from the dead man and shot into her Father, sending him staggering backwards.

Samanthiel screamed, rushing down to the hall below, stopping as she entered the main hall. The floor was slick and slippery with the life blood of dozens of soldiers. In the middle her Father stood facing away, with his head bowed as if in prayer.

"Daddy?" Samanthiel said tentatively.

Her Father began to turn ever so slowly.

Samanthiel's heartbeat quickened, and a watery sickness churned in her stomach. Finally their eyes locked, but it was not the loving familiar eyes of her Father; they were cold and dead, his handsome face twisted into a feral snarl.

Heavy sobs wracked her young frame as Samanthiel raised her loaded crossbow on shaky arms.

"Sssssaaaammmmyyyy...," her Father hissed, stepping on the bodies as he began moving swiftly towards her.

"Daddy...forgive me..."

She squeezed the trigger and the quarrel flew true, striking him in the chest. Samanthiel turned and fled, shrieking in mindless terror.

Chapter 40

Lillith stooped folding her jet-black, feathered wings behind her back as she lifted a large, dark chunk of shattered stone. Whispering a magical incantation, she blew upon it with a crystalline breath. The rock shimmered and dissolved into a glittering cloud of particles that rose and swirled in a vortex around her. When the light dimmed, the rock reformed into a perfect, figure hugging, black armour.

She turned to Belthor, who still stood where she had left him, and pointed to the remaining two standing stones. They were inscribed with the final two words of power – La Ohlam and Amen.

"Over there," she pointed at the stones.

Belthor turned without question and moved to stand between the obelisks.

"Forever...so be it...,"she whispered, raising her arm, sending a ball of dark energy shooting across the room. It hit Belthor in the chest and his clothes fell away in flames, leaving a snake of darkness to twist to each wrist and hold him fast to each of the stones.

The red-hot agony of the of the burning cleansed the hypnotic hold that Lillith had placed him under, the pain bringing back his senses.

He writhed against his black bonds, struggling in vain till exhaustion claimed the last of his strength and he slumped, hanging by his wrists.

Lailoken began to laugh at Belthor's predicament. Stepping close, he gripped him by the chin and lifting his head roughly, staring deep into his weary eyes.

"You have lost, Servant of the rock Goddess. By now the assassin, Snare will have destroyed your beloved Grandson and his female companion, and will be returning to Darkhaven with the Angel Raziel's magical book. Then my Mistress will destroy your Gods one after the other, before this pathetic world's end, and a new dawn can be created."

"Don't be so sure of your assassin, Demon." Belthor said with gritted teeth, struggling to keep the fact that it was his own son finally standing before him from clouding his judgement.

"You and your damned Angel will... be... defeated. Remember the...prophecy...,"

A painful spasm of coughing wracked his old frame.

Lillith pushed Lailoken out of the way and faced the old mage, dark rage shining in her eyes, her raven hair flaring and crackling with dangerous energy. She snarled, placing a hand on each of the standing stones. Dark magic flowed, the runes etched into the surface of each stone transforming into symbols older than time.

Belthor gasped in pain as the floor at his feet became slick with ice. Uttering a harsh syllable, and giving a fierce nod, the Angel stepped back.

A bright light encompassed Belthor and in moments he was encased to his waist in blistering ice. Belthor hung in terrible torment, numbness spreading up his stomach.

Lillith gave a low chuckle, bending to pick up a shard of stone. She blew upon the rock and it began to glow, turning malleable in her fist. Rolling it back and forth between her palms, she sharpened the lengthening stone into a lethal point. She snarled, baring her teeth and ran her black tongue down the spike's razor length.

Lillith held the tip of the spike before Belthor's face, and hissed, "Waken!"

Belthor raised himself slowly, focus returning to his bleary eyes. He looked at the glowing tip and began to weep; knowing what lay ahead.

She lowered the stone till the point rested against the centre of his chest.

Belthor's shallow breath rapidly increased.

She began to slowly push the spike into his body, it pierced his skin and a single drop of his blood fell.

Belthor's world folded in on itself, as the spike slid through his solar plexus energy centre. His soul was expelled and hung in midair, the silver cord now attached to the tip of the evil stone.

Lillith looked up at Belthor's hovering spirit and smiled. She reached out and snapped the end off the stone, and tucked the broken piece into her armour.

"Come, my faithful servant, we have a world to destroy." She said light-heartedly, taking Lailoken in tow, turning and heading for the stairs.

Chapter 41

Jack stood on the bank of the river Ulfen, the massive bridge towers of Ulfenspan stretching into the distance. This was Ulfenspan *before* Belthor sank it beneath the roaring river water, recreated perfectly by Samanthiel's subconscious mind, her afterlife and her prison.

He stared in awe at the first tower rising majestically from the foam, craning his neck as his eyes followed the bridge-city above to the second tower.

The magic swirling within his soul guided him through the main gate and up into the first tower. A dreadful scene of death and violence greeted him in the main hall. A deformed Demon was studded with arrows and the bodies of the towerguard who had been possessed now lay scattered around the room dead to the last man.

Suddenly the scene shimmered and melted into a white light, before reforming once again to the point before the Demon arrived. Guards formed ranks as the reports of an approaching creature reached the handsome captain.

Jack walked up to the man who was obviously Samanthiel's Father, "I have come to take Samanthiel back."

The man turned and walked right through Jack as if he was not there.

I was not here, not at the time that this happened, Jack thought.

Jack could only watch as the Demon was killed and the cycle of destruction began again. As the battle died down, Jack was drawn to the high balcony overlooking the hall.

Samanthiel stood there, *she is so beautiful,* he thought. Jack had never seen her dressed in finery with long hair. He shot up and stopped beside her.

"Sam! It's me, Jack!"

She ignored him, eyes wide and wild.

"Sam! Come on, look at me!"

She called out to her father, and rushed past Jack down the stairs. Jack followed, frantically trying to think of what to do next.

He was stunned when she fired the crossbow at her father, but realised that it had to be done. It finally sunk in and he understood her deep rooted hate for the Demons and the overwhelming need to destroy every last one of them.

As Samanthiel ran off screaming, the scene changed and the devastation began again.

*

Jack rose high into the air above the city, floating on the bright breeze. Below he could see the citizens fleeing into the second tower, and Samanthiel moving against the tide of humanity.

There is only one person who will be able to break the cycle, he thought.

Jack willed himself to the tower captain, Samanthiel's Father. The bridge below vanished, replaced by a shining ribbon of the clearest water. The Celestial River of the afterlife flowed through lush green lands. Tranquil settlements lining both banks, as far as the eye could see.

Jack was drawn to a small town where the houses were built on small stone piers jutting into the water, each having a slipway and boat tied at anchor.

This would be a fantastic place to spend eternity, Jack thought.

The door opened and a man walked out, Jack recognised Samanthiel's father; though he looked younger and fitter than her most recent memories.

"Well met, Jack the Hawk!" he said offering a strong hand, which Jack took and shook.

"I am Jason, former Captain of tower one."

"You...You know me?"

He nodded and smiled. "Your name and exploits are legendary, here on the shining shores, Jack. Ulfner and the Angels have seen to that. I have waited for this day for many years! Take me to my Sammy, please. I can help her."

"Years? You have been...err dead... for less than one year."

Samanthiel's Father laughed easily.

"Time is not an issue here, Jack. A single day in the physical can take many years here, and likewise a moment here can stretch forever!"

*

Jack and Jason stood on the high balcony watching. Jason watched in amusement as he and his men fought the Demon, then each other.

"Yes. That is just how it happened. Isn't it amazing, the power of the Higher Mind."

Jack frowned. "Higher Mind?"

"We all have a Higher mind, Jack. It is linked to the creator herself, she learns from each experience we endure in every lifetime and we grow as beings; stronger in the soul, climbing towards the next stage of mankind's evolution."

Jack was confused, *each life time? Return and grow? Evolution?*

"You are the evolution, Jack; you and your family. One day, everyone will have Changeling abilities... everyone."

Samanthiel burst into the top of the tower, grasping the crossbow tightly. She locked eyes with her father, and she blinked, then frowned.

"Daddy? The...the Demon."

Jason stepped close to her and enfolded her in his arms, kissing the large tears that welled in her beautiful eyes.

"Shh, Sammy. It is over. We are all safe now."

Jack swallowed, a lump in his throat.

"Jack is here to take you back, Sammy. He needs you."

"Jack...here?" she said distantly; confused.

He nodded. "You were taken before your allotted time, by the dark assassin, Garan Snare, and Jack has come to take you back to the physical realm."

Samanthiel's eyes widened as clarity returned and she cried out, "Snare! He killed me! I remember now."

She turned to Jack and smiled. "Jack...," she frowned. "I...don't...think I want to go back."

Jack blinked. "I need you, Sam," he whispered hoarsely.

Jason placed a fatherly hand on her shoulder, and pushed her gently towards Jack, "Go Sammy, there are still many Demons and worse still to tackle..."

At the mere mention of Demons, Samanthiel's eyes narrowed and she automatically reached for her sword Nemesis, but it was not there. "Demons...I must stop them."

She turned to her Father and gave him a long hard hug, burying her face in his shirt.

Jason nodded to Jack and let his daughter go.

"I love you, Samanthiel. I will be here the next time you decide to visit..." he chuckled, "and then you can stay for longer!"

Samanthiel turned to Jack and reached for his hand. As their fingers intertwined an electric warmth passed through Jack's palm into hers. Suddenly her grip tightened painfully, and she drew a sharp breath, then exhaled deeply. Then repeated the strange breathing again. Slowly the city of Ulfenspan dissolved around them, and they fell into the darkness of the void.

Jack willed himself back to the physical world, and moments later the bright doorframe zoomed towards them and stopped.

"You have returned unscathed, and shared of yourself," declared the booming voice of the Watcher at the Threshold.

"I have...I think..." Jack said, unsure of what had passed between them.

"Then pass, Jack the Hawk, pass, Samanthiel Demonslayer."

Jack and Samanthiel popped through the door and found themselves back in the temple with Gaia still standing guard.

Suddenly Samanthiel shot past him and rejoined her physical body in a silent burst of light. Jack had to avert his eyes as her aura pulsed first golden then green, shining brilliantly. Moments later he popped back into his own body and opened his eyes.

Samanthiel lay on the ground before him, a rosy glow burning her cheeks. Then her eyes widened in shock as she noticed that her shirt was open, hastily buttoning the bloody garment. She sat up swiftly, the flush of embarrassment spreading down her neck and chest.

"I didn't...I mean, I did...but," Jack began, his own cheeks burning.

Samanthiel smiled and sat up, placing a finger across his lips to silence him. She removed her hand and leant forward and gave Jack a small kiss on the cheek, whispering, "Thank you for saving me, Jack."

Chapter 42

The Darkhaven army was in turmoil, driven into a righteous crusade that turned brother against brother, father against son. Then the Lord Lailoken had split the camp in half, screaming orders to destroy everything. The men whispered quiet mutiny. They whispered of returning home and forgetting, driving the memories of the atrocities they had committed in the name of the Lord's Riznar and Lailoken.

But their Lord Lailoken had returned, and he was not alone.

*

Lailoken called the camp to muster and the Angel Lillith cast her dark eye over the troops. Unfolding her wings, she gave a slow regular flap and rose gracefully into the air. She captivated their minds; her dark magic sweeping all thoughts of desertion and dissention from the camp, bending and binding every soul to her will.

As one, everyone knelt bowing in acquiescence.

She landed gracefully next to Lailoken.

"You," she pointed directly at one of the men, "approach."

The soldier rose like an automaton, eyes glazed, devoid of intelligence. He stumbled slackly towards Lillith, coming to a wobbly halt at her side. She gripped the man by the throat and tightened her fist slightly, raising him till his feet dangled. He choked slightly his breath coming in a slight rasp, yet he made no complaint.

"Ragathazar, Ethrazar, Yothsogoth," Lillith's voice was guttural and raw, her beauty twisting hideously as she spoke the horrible curse.

A black flame burned the unfortunate soldier, blistering his skin, the flesh crisping and splitting.

Still he made no sound.

The flame consumed him, till his body became a dangling black inferno. Lillith held firm as the body in her iron fist, twisted and burned. Finally she dropped the incinerated body onto the grass, the flames dying along with the man.

She raised a smoking fist to the heavens, again crying out, "Astaroth...return to me."

Thunder cracked and a dark orb fell from the heavens, shooting into the body at her feet. It split open, an over long scaly arm snaking from the raw flesh, followed by a muscular shoulder and a gore slimed, red-eyed, face.

She knelt and pulled the Demon tenderly from the body. Her first child was reborn, claimed from the circle of life that Danu, her sworn enemy, had condemned him and his brethren to.

"Sweet Astaroth," she knelt cradled the steaming monster, as it gasped a first breath.

"Mother!" It managed, through an over full mouth of fangs, glowing eyes widening in recognition.

Lillith rose, helping her creation to it's feet. The monster now hulked over her, expanding and filling out with each passing moment.

"Feed and grow strong, Astaroth," she ordered.

The Demon plunged forward into the ranks, noisily devouring a few of the Darkhaven nobles.

Lillith watched intently for a few moments before turning to Lailoken. "There are not enough here to return all my children to this plane."

"There is a large gathering of cattle across the river, where we were burned by the detestable Darkbane and his Angels, but this river is uncrossable..."

Lillith's eyes narrowed into black slits, "Uncrossable? We shall remedy that."

Lillith led Lailoken through the crowd of immobile troops, past the multitude of tents, down towards the roaring waters of the river Ulfen.

She stopped close to the bank, facing the river. Slowly she raised her clawed hands to the sky, screeching in a tone that pierced and grated painfully.

Lailoken staggered as a blast of ice-cold air swept outwards from Lillith. The stones and grass at her feet froze, furry frost forming in moments, radiating outwards in all directions.

The water began to freeze in a spreading semicircle, a thin crust of ice forming, that rapidly thickened, crackling and crunching noisily.

She turned to Lailoken, speaking in a tone that left no room for questions. "You will retrieve Raziel's tome, and bring it directly to me."

Lailoken nodded, dropped his robe and gave his Changeling cry, transforming once again into a huge eagle. Taking flight, he circled the camp, leaving his mistress behind, as he winged his way swiftly back towards Darkhaven.

Chapter 43

Jack stooped by Garan Snare's lifeless body. The assassin had died, reaching in vain for the ruby at his throat, and Jack had to prise open his stiff, cold fingers to retrieve the magical jewel.

Samanthiel stood shakily, the memories of her afterlife experience fading to dream. She watched emotionless as Jack pulled the charm from the assassin's damaged neck. A churning and swirling began in her innards; something was happening but she felt strangely detached and unable to say anything.

Jack, I...I don't...feel...well, she thought.

Jack turned instantly, concern on his face, "What did you say, Sam? Are you unwell?"

She tried to shake her head, but continued swaying till slowly she crumpled to the floor, in a dead faint.

Jack leapt to her side, catching her before she hit the stone. "Sam," he cried, shaking her gently.

"She is fighting your gift, Jack." Gaia said from the shadow.

Jack looked up at the old woman, "My...gift?"

Half hidden in shadow, Gaia's eyes glittered. "She is changing, Jack. She is ...becoming."

Jack stared down at the girl on the floor, his own heart thudding rapidly, as a ripple spread over her creamy skin. She arched her back and gave a low moan as patches of skin broke open and small black scales slithered into view. Her nose seemed to flatten and spread into slits, as her transformation sped up.

Gaia knelt by her head and wiped the sheen of sweat from her fevered brow. Samanthiel's eyelids fluttered open and Jack gasped; her eyes had turned smoky yellow, with a slit of pale blue for a pupil. He shuddered as memories and sensations of the pain of his own recent transformation came flooding back to him.

Jack stooped, lifting Samanthiel easily. Her body was roasting hot, angular bones seemed to be squirming beneath her overstretched skin.

"Wh...what's happening...to...to me, Jack?" She gasped, the flicker of a dark, forked-tongue showing.

Jack didn't know what to say, but instinct took over and he whispered magically, "Sleep," and her eyelids slid closed once again.

Gaia led the way as they left the chamber and moved out of the temple, through the forest and back towards the village.

*

Samanthiel spent the night on a simple straw pallet in the middle of Gaia's hut, shivering with a terrible fever, sweat plastering her remaining blond hair to her head. As they had travelled back from the temple, tatters of skin had fallen in damp scraps. She was no longer human; covered from head to toe in glistening black scales, and with each wheezing breath, smoke rose from her flared nostrils.

Jack crouched as he entered the hut, carrying the sword, Nemesis. He leant over Samanthiel and carefully lifted her arm, placing the scabbard across her body, lowering her hand onto the hilt. Her dark, clawed fingertips closed instinctively around the grip, and the Dragon engraving flared with crimson flames.

Instantly she opened her eyes, and sat bolt upright, the sword helping her to focus her racing mind. She saw her arms and body and screamed; a gout of flames shooting from her mouth.

"Sam!" Jack cried, "don't worry. Let it happen."

Samanthiel's head whipped around and she gave Jack a wild-eyed glare. She gripped Jack's arm, the talons drawing points of blood.

"What, Jack? Let...what...happen?"

"You are changing, Sam," Jack said, ignoring the pain of her iron grip. "I have shared of myself with you, it was the price I had to pay to bring you back." He paused. "You are becoming a Changeling, Sam."

Samanthiel screamed and let go of Jack's arm, swinging Nemesis straight at him. Jack automatically raised his arm in defence, barely managing to shout, *"Sheild!"*

The two magical weapons clashed with a flash of hot energy. Samanthiel looked down at her naked body. Her breast and stomach were covered in thick overlapping plates of shining black scale; while hundreds of small, dark scales covered her arms and legs.

Jack scrabbled back as Samanthiel leapt to her feet, eyes narrowing to sizzling slits. She snarled and dived towards him, as he backed towards the entrance, the pair tumbling out into the clearing.

Small figures melted into the early morning shadows, as the pair rose, circling each other, breathing heavily. Jack's mind raced, as she lunged again. Her sword sliced high, catching him in the shoulder, he gave a grunt of pain as the blood flowed and he dropped his shield from numbed fingers.

"Cease!" Gaia boomed from her doorway. She was small and frail, yet left them both in no doubt that she wielded great power.

Jack staggered back a step and held a hand to the open wound, stemming the blood loss.

"There has been enough killing this day, Samanthiel." Gaia spoke. "That boiling in your blood is the Dragon within you. It is trying to break free and stretch its wings."

Samanthiel looked down at her forearm and hand, flexing her muscles experimentally.

"It does feel...strong." She looked back at Jack who stood silent, an expression of sorrow on his face. "We will have words about this later, Jack." She struggled with the words for her mouth was filling with sharp, pointed teeth.

Jack nodded, stepping cautiously towards her. He reached out, placing his hand on her arm. The Changeling power within him churned and writhed, recognising the similar energy a skin's breadth away.

Samanthiel dropped Nemesis to the ground, the Changeling words springing into her mind. They started as a whisper that rapidly ended in a scream.

"Dragon Fly... Dragon Eye... Dragon Be... Dragon Me!"

She hunched forwards and fell to the ground, landing on all fours, panting and gasping as her bones snapped and crunched noisily. Birds flew and the forest grew silent as her terrible screams echoed between the trees. Her head jerked from side to side as the bones popped and grew in her lengthening neck. Two nubs formed at the top of her spiky spine, rapidly expanding; becoming a pair of large dark wings. Finally a whiplash tail stretched and snaked, growing till the transformation was complete.

Jack stood in silent awe; she had not passed out, his admiration for her endurance and strength grew.

Samanthiel rose to her full height stretching her serpentine neck to full length, roaring with all her newfound might.

"By the Goddess! That hurt." Samanthiel cried in a loud telepathic voice. Jack laughed, despite his painful wound. Now he knew how his Uncle Lupin felt that night in the forest, when he first changed.

He channelled some of the forest's growing power into a small healing spell. A tiny sphere of glowing green rose from the earth, dancing from his fingertips. The light bobbed up his arm and settled on the wound, forming a liquid patch. In a few moments the throbbing pain faded, leaving only a thin white line on his shoulder.

Gaia strode purposefully forward and placed a gnarled hand on Samanthiel's sleek neck and turned to Jack. "You have come here and I have taken you to Raziel's Book. I watched as you freed Samanthiel's soul from eternal torment and shared your Changeling powers with her. Now I ask one boon in return."

"I will do anything I can," he promised.

Gaia reached out with a thin arm, touching his shoulder, linking between him and the dark scaled Dragon.

"The mighty power that is hidden within the dark folds of your mind can help my children, Jack. So before you use that dark jewel and go on to fulfil your destiny, please help me to change them."

Jack felt a stirring, deep within his mind; bright strands of thought weaving into the mesh of a magical idea. His breathing deepened and a powerful surge of energy circulated into a loop, flowing from the earth, through Samanthiel and Gaia, back through him into the ground again.

A hazy glow formed around the magical trio as the words came to the front of his mind, and Jack's eyes transformed into liquid gold pools of light as the words came of their own accord.

"Come forth children of the sacred forest."

Dozens of small shapes began appearing from the shade between the trees, some squat, others lanky and thin, all misshapen. They shuffled nervously from the shadows, forming a semicircle, till the clearing was filled.

"This forest has been branded 'cursed and haunted', but this day it will end. Now you will all choose a permanent shape and the Changeling ways shall be yours alone, completely under your control." Jack's voice was deep and rich, full of reassuring authority.

A ripple of astonishment spread visibly outwards as dozens of shining heads bobbed up and down, an excited chirping chatter buzzing through the crowd.

"Choose and Change!" He shouted magically, the ground shaking in a violent tremor as a blinding wall of light swept over the gathered creatures.

A fearful cry rose from their throats as the spell took hold. One by one, Gaia's children began to change.

Chapter 44

The elderly houseman wound the silver wire around Lord Ness's hair, binding it in a thick tail. He fastened his cloak over the worn steel armour, clasping the Dragon-shaped pin at his throat and strapping his large sword across his back.

"Thank you, Fredrick." Ness said.

"Good luck with the barbarians, Sir."

"Thank you again, Fredrick." He laughed good-naturedly, "But I am glad to say the Lord Grim seems a worthy leader for the Grim folk."

Opening the front door Ness winced in the early morning light; but glad his pounding headache had reduced to a slight inconvenience.

*

A large contingent of Grimswadian troops had arrived the previous evening, led by the new Lord Grim, Sigurd himself, declaring the mountain passes clear of the remaining Demon scourge.

At the welcoming feast Sigurd's bard had sung a stirring song of bravery and wild adventure, entitled – 'An Ode to the Fair Warrior Maiden and Her Dragon.'

Ness demanded a full retelling of Sigurd's sad tale and the heroic feats of Jack and Samanthiel. In turn, Sigurd had listened to the tales of woe from the distant Darkhaven and the far shore of the River Ulfen. His surprise turning to anger at the capture of Jack's Grandfather, the anger turning to a drunken, heroic banter as he swore a blood oath of friendship, promising to stand to the last man at Lord Ness's side against the fallen Angel and her army.

Using a psychic mindlink, Alvor had suggested bringing troops to the river, suspecting that dark magic could move the

Darkhaven army across the water. As they hugged and parted for the night, Sigurd promised his men would be ready to march at first light.

Lord Ness had left the revellers in the small hours, with the threat of an early rise in the morning looming close.

*

Lord Ness and his troops stood in well ordered ranks outside the walls, north of the city, as the morning sun crested the distant, forested hilltops.

Two hundred heavily armoured, mounted knights, led by the veteran Captain Reed, and two thousand light infantry foot soldiers, their ranks swollen mostly with raw recruits, waited patiently.

The knights were a well trained but fairly recently form-ed unit, recruited mainly from the sons and daughters of the city's wealthier citizenry; for each member had to buy their own arms, armour and warhorse.

As he approached, Thunder whinnied and tossed his long black mane. Lord Ness took the reins from his young stable-boy, patting his steed's nose lovingly.

"Help me up please, John." Ness said to the lad.

The strapping lad, latticed his fingers, bending as Ness lifted his polished, black boot, and hefted himself into the high saddle.

"Sir!" A girl's voice rang out. Ness twisted in his saddle, as a striking horse galloped through the gate. It was a beaut-iful chestnut stallion, tall and strong with a brilliant white star between his eyes, topped with a figure, dressed in slightly over-sized armour.

"Lord Ness," she cried breathlessly, lifting the visor of her helmet, pulling it off as her horse came to a prancing halt. The morning breeze caught the long strands of blown gold. "Take me with you! I am the best rider in Ness!"

Ness frowned, then his face softened as he recognised his chief stable girl, Ann. The girl was tall and slender, sitting solidly in her saddle despite the cumbersome armour; the years of mucking out the stables had seen her well toned muscles grow strong. She had protested with wild fire in her two-tone eyes when he had denied her a place in the mounted regiment, and it seemed she had disobeyed the order to stay put.

"Ann, you are right." Ness began. "You are the best rider, but you have not trained enough with the sword and lance."

She was about to protest, when Ness raised a gauntlet.

"When we return, I want you to enlist in the combat school, and maybe then we will have the pleasure of your company in the ranks. Is that fair enough?"

Ann flushed red, bit her lip, nodding reluctantly before tugging the reins and turning her horse. "Yes Sir, forgive me."

Then with a small kick of her heels and click of her tongue. "Home, Star!"

Ness looked after the returning stable hand with a fond smile, when a clamour began to ring out over the city, as the growing parade of Grimswadian troops marched from various inns and taverns across the commercial district. Some still dripped water from the drenching used to revive them from alcohol fuelled slumber.

"Line up lads!" Sigurd roared, striding through the gates. He marched up, standing almost as tall as Ness on his horse, his famous stone axe strapped across his back.

He stretched, cracking his joints noisily. "A good looking warband, my Lord."

He eyed the lined ranks appreciatively, as the rest of his own troops strolled nonchalantly to form a crowd beside him, their huge swords, axes and maces hefted easily over broad shoulders.

Ness smiled, he like Sigurd, believing him to be a solid and dependable ally. Sigurd's father, the previous Lord Grim, had been a distant and slightly suspicious figure that had never crossed the mountains in all the years that Ness had served, till his untimely demise at the hands of the assassins.

"Captain Reed," Ness called.

Reed rode close. "Sir?"

"We will march east to the river. Send some scouts ahead to find young Lupin. His eyes and ears are keener than ours." Reed nodded, turned his steed and began bellowing orders.

Sigurd shielded his eyes from the bright sun, and took a swig from his flask, "Damn it Ness, your ale is terrible, but your wine is so good."

Ness laughed. "Lord Grim, you should never mix the grape and the grain! But I seem to recall that it took you several flagons of each to come to that decision."

Sigurd broke into a loud laugh, wiping the red wine that had dribbled into his thick beard.

Ness trotted out into the field, wheeled his horse around and faced the gathered forces.

"Soldiers of Ness and men of Grimswade," he called out in a loud clear voice. "We face dark times ahead. We ride and march east into an uncertain future. We will face an enemy that may not be easily defeated, but face them we must! Some of you stood here less than a year ago, when we faced a terrible Demon army. We all lost friends that dark night, but we endured with the aid of a young lad and his angelic friends. Now a greater threat is approaching; a wave of darkness threatens to fall over the land and extinguish all the light. Will you march with me and become a beacon of light in this coming darkness?"

"I will fight!" A single voice from the ranks rang out and was quickly copied till the troops, from both cities, all chanted in unison.

Tears welled in Ness's old eyes, and he turned in the saddle and pointing eastwards, spurring Thunder into a trot, crying, "For the Goddess, for the Light!"

Chapter 45

Lailoken soared through the clouds high over the deserted city of Darkhaven. He spiralled around the high plaza and High Council building, landing lightly on Riznar's balcony.

In a dark flash of transformation, he stood naked in the morning sunlight. He stretched tall, arching his back, giving a roar of triumph; delighted by the dark magic his angelic mistress had returned to him. The dying echo reverberated over the empty city far below

A rumble then a cursing clatter sounded through the shattered window. "M...master? Is...is that you?"

Lailoken stepped into the room, the smell of rotten fruit and the stench of stale urine and unwashed flesh was sweet perfume to the Demon, and he took a deep sniff savouring the foul odour.

"Riznar, the time has come," his voice was deep and clear,

A filthy, dishevelled Riznar came stumbling blindly through the litter and waste towards the voice of his master. His bloated face was blistered and raw, the skin dyed a bright fluorescent green. He had survived on the remnants of his fruit platter and wine flask and was now weak with the lack of fresh water.

Lailoken pulled on his robe, no longer requiring the golden mask. He placed a large hand on Riznar's head and uttered a few harsh words. The green stain faded and vanished, Riznar's sight restored. The fat man fell to his knees, staring in awe at his renewed dark master.

"It is done, Riznar. My shadow Mistress is now free, and with the Book she shall defeat the Gods and even challenge the creator herself! Her rule of darkness will be unstoppable."

Lailoken scanned the room; there was no sign of the assassin and the precious book.

"Where is Snare? Has he not returned?"

Riznar shook his head. "He has not, master."

"Then find him!" He commanded, slamming the palm of his hand into Riznar's forehead with a dark flash of magic. The shock sent him sprawling, and his soul flew free of his body. He bobbed awkwardly like an over-sized balloon; it had been many years since he had had the inclination to practice astral travel.

With a thought, he shot out through the wall and began his trip westwards. In a few moments he passed the dark Angel and the growing Demon army massed on the shore of the half frozen river. Her dark aura seemed to absorb the energy and devour the light from the surrounding people and land.

She is truly a being of great darkness, Riznar thought in awe.

Soon he passed over Lord Ness and the column of troops snaking though the hills heading towards the river, barely giving it a glance as he sped onwards over the Grimswadian mountain pastures.

He swept past the mountain city of Grimswade, glowing as if each house was constructed with bricks of fiery crystal. Riznar felt uneasy, the city seemed to radiate joy and well-being, not the dread and sadness he expected from a suppressed kingdom, overthrown and living in subjugation. He decided to investigate this after he discovered Snare's where-abouts.

Soon he slowed to a bobbing hover over the brilliant green glow of the deep forest. Thinking of the book, he began a slow spiralling descent through the towering treetops, passing through the foliage and thick branches, floating into the village clearing.

His senses were immediately assaulted by a rainbow sea of light. The area below was awash with the soul-colour of brilliant auras, making it difficult for Riznar to focus his thoughts.

Then his astral attention was drawn to a trio of bright beings that outshone the rest of the creatures in the clearing.

Chapter 46

Gaia gazed up into the trees with narrowed eyes, instantly spotting Riznar's dark soul hovering beneath the canopy. Her wizened face contorted in disgust and she spat on the ground.

Swiftly she began to mutter an incantation, her fingers twitching and pointing from bough to bole; limb to branch; tree to tree; crisscrossing the clearing with an enchanted web of light.

Samanthiel spotted Gaia's actions, whipping her monstrous, black head up into the leafy branches snapping her gleaming, razor teeth ineffectually at the puzzling shadow.

The shade shot sideways, colliding with an invisible barrier, then back again into a similar immovable obstruction; trapped like a dark wasp in a jar of light.

"What have we here?" Gaia said, lowering the cage with a slight flick of her wrist.

Riznar floated, unable to escape, anger and fear swirling in the dark eddies of his aura, radiating deep shades of purple and black.

"Seems we have a dark spy in our midst. Checking up on your failed assassin, eh?" Gaia cackled. "He is over there." She pointed at a small handcart, overloaded with a black lump wrapped in a cloak.

Jack sensed the being floating, and after tuning his senses was aghast to discover it was his Grandfather's old adversary. Belthor had warned Jack of his enemy, Riznar, and his suspicions about his involvement with Lailoken's disappearance.

A swirling rage boiled in Jack's stomach and thoughts of bloody revenge leapt to mind; for this was the spirit of the horrible man who was responsible for the assassin that had taken Belthor, killed Sigurd's father and Samanthiel.

Gaia appeared at his side, placing a cool, reassuring hand upon his arm.

"Drive these dark thoughts from your head, Jack, for anger and fury harm the soul. You need to get ready to use the magical stone the assassin carried. Please help change Samanthiel back into human form, and I shall hold this miscreant's spirit captive for now."

Gaia reached into her robe and pulled out several small wooden totems, shaped like forest creatures and birds. She planted them into the hard packed earth of the clearing and closed her eyes, concentrating hard.

As Jack knelt and prepared to try and change Samanthiel back into human form, he noticed the small symbols glowing then begin to move as if alive. The small animals circled the cage faster and faster till they became a blur of light. Time seemed to slow down, and within the prison the dark soul froze.

Gaia heaved a tired sigh. "Have you not done it yet, Jack?"

Samanthiel lowered her snout to the ground and waited as Gaia stood behind Jack and placed a hand upon his shoulder. Jack turned to Gaia, with a frown, "I don't know how to change her back. I mean it is different for me. I just concentrate and think myself back. How do I actually change her?"

As he babbled to Gaia, there was a soft light and a gentle rush of wind, and when he turned Samanthiel stood there, quite naked, swaying and still slightly dazed. She gave a small shriek of embarrassed fright, covering her body with her arms before dashing over and pulling the cloak from Snare's body, wrapping her nudity as fast as possible.

Jack's jaw hung open and his face burned. Samanthiel shot him a warning look, followed by a smug smile. "I managed without your help, thank you." She said primly, then she frowned and gave a petulant cry, "I wanted to fly!"

Gaia laughed warmly. "You will fly aplenty in the future, Samanthiel. It seems you have picked up more than just Jack's Changeling ways. Look in the back of my home, there are several items of armour and clothing, left by the Grimswadians as tribute to the Gods in ancient times."

Jack and Samanthiel disappeared into the hut, while Gaia considered what to do about Riznar.

*

Jack adjusted the old leather strapping on the ornately engraved breast plate as Samanthiel breathed in.

"Tighter!" she said with a grimace.

They found the small storeroom packed to the gunnels with assorted armour and treasures, and enough gold to run a kingdom. It seemed that in the past the superstitious Grimswadians had given generously.

Both were dressed in an odd assortment of armour and clothing, Jack wore a silver scalemail shirt and an armoured kilt of overlapping metal plate. While Samanthiel chose an expensive, gold embossed, leather breastplate, and leather breeks sewn with hundreds of circular discs of shimmering steel.

"Turn around," said Jack, as he helped her with the buckle of her sword belt.

As she turned back, she caught his gaze.

Jack swallowed, looking away. Her stern features softened into a smile, and she pulled gently on the fuzzy growth on his chin.

"Jack, I am sorry for overreacting...I haven't..."

"That's fine, Sam. Don't worry..." He blurted out, interrupting.

She frowned again, annoyed. "I am trying to say thank you, Jack! You did something brave for me, and I now have an amazing gift. I think it is time for us to go and say goodbye to Gaia, and use this bloody gem."

Jack sat for a moment, thinking over a plan, before making sure Samanthiel knew what he intended to do once they used the gem.

*

Jack hugged the old woman, and swallowed. a lump rising in his throat. "Gaia..."

Gaia shook her head. "Go Jack. Save my Brother and send the foul Demon back where he belongs. We will do what we can to help you from here."

"I think you'd better get clear from here, Gaia. This jewel can cause quite an explosion."

Samanthiel took Jack by the hand as Gaia and the creatures of the haunted forest vanished silently into the woods.

"Ready?" he asked.

"Go for it!" Samanthiel's beautiful eyes sparkled with excitement.

Jack reached for the red gem and spoke one word.

"Home!"

Chapter 47

Lailoken paced back and forth in Riznar's apartment, impatient and angry; he did not like to keep his Mistress waiting. He glared at the fallen figure of Riznar, who lay where he fell. He looked dead; his sagging face ghostly and pale, his bloated body vacant, the spirit gone.

A hurricane wind swept into the room, billowing the sumptuous drapes. A blinding flash blazed in the centre of the room. It dimmed to leave, not the dark assassin, but two armoured figures, crouched, ready for battle.

"The Dragonboy...and...a little girl!" Lailoken's surprised cry ended in scorn.

"Prepare to die, Demon!" Samanthiel cried shrilly.

Jack let go of Samanthiel's hand and cried, *"Sword,"* as Samanthiel dived into a roll, rising on top of the cracked seeing table with her bright sword, Nemesis, drawn.

A deep chuckle echoed from the far side of the room. A quick scan of the room, and Jack took in the imposing, red-robed figure striding purposefully towards them, and the prone pile of flesh that was Riznar.

Lailoken raised a hand wreathed in dark fire, spitting harsh syllables. A lance of flame swept across the room, aimed at Jack. He swept his sword up parrying the lethal attack. Flames flared brilliantly as the dark fire was shattered into a greasy black rain.

Samanthiel leapt high, sweeping her sword at Lailoken's head. He gave her a cursory glance and with a nod, she flew backwards slamming into the wall, where she sank to the ground, winded.

Jack used the distraction.

"Staff," he said.

The sword elongated into a long rod tipped with balls of green flame. Holding the weapon with both hands, Jack closed his eyes, feeling for the power of Raziel's book. He could almost feel the personalities of the deities surfacing and guiding him.

Knowledge is power, he thought.

Suddenly he knew how to remove the Demon's dark magic, and a plan surfaced into his mind. The surging knowledge almost twisted his skeleton within his skin. Jack's spirit soared, and he felt as if he was riding upon the crest of a mighty tidal wave as the colossal power of the drifting continents, and pent up fury of the erupting volcano formed into one single magical incantation, "Yahweh - Adonai!"

Lailoken stopped mid-stride. His dead eyes widened in surprise, confusion and fear. He felt the gift of dark magic evaporate, and intense paralysis begin to seize every thread of muscle.

"The Book! You have the book, Changeling! My...Mistress...will..." He barely managed to speak before his jaw muscles tightened, silencing him.

Jack opened his eyes and fixed Lailoken with a steely gaze. Lailoken's eyes narrowed as Jack slowly lowered himself to the floor, folding his legs and settling, seemingly unconcerned.

Sam! I hope she's not hurt! Jack panicked inwardly, not wanting to show the Demon his emotions. He willed himself to rise free from his body and without a pause, his spirit shot across the room and into Lailoken's body.

His perception shifted and the world appeared to implode as he found himself inside the warped and possessed mind of his father.

*

Samanthiel groaned and shook her head. Her blurry vision cleared to reveal a bizarre sight. The gaunt Demon seemed frozen, one arm raised, the clawed hand pointing at the air above Jack, who was sitting eyes closed and cross-legged, with a flaming staff resting across his knees.

She rose and began moving slowly towards the pair. Nemesis glowed brighter as she neared the immobile Lailoken. She was relieved to see Jack's chest rise and fall in a slow, steady rhythm, whilst Lailoken seemed to be turning a strange shade of blue.

Chapter 48

Jack found himself standing on a desolate wintry hilltop, beneath a churning, pendulous, cloud-filled sky. He overlooked a snow topped labyrinth of gigantic proportions; the massive stone maze covering the land in every direction.

The stark, jet-black, stone wall was broken down in only one place, just below, and something red caught his attention at the entrance.

As he approached the damaged wall, he stopped short; for amongst the dark rubble a single sheet of blood-red paper was flapping crazily in the keening wind.

Everything felt solid and real, in Lailoken's mindscape. He clambered over the jagged boulders and found the paper hooked on a sharp corner.

Jack read the note and was shaken by the single word plea, 'Help!'

He quickly climbed the pile of stones and slid down the scree into the high sided maze. The narrow corridor stretched away into a point in the distance, with offshoot turns every so often.

Jack began a quick trot, following a single track of small footprints leading off into the distance. The prints doubled back at the next junction, and led off in two directions. Jack turned left onto the new passage. The moaning wind grew stronger, funnelling between the high walls, till each step was a labour.

Hold on, Jack thought angrily to himself, *this is not real. This is all in his mind.*

The howling wind died instantly and an unnerving, still-ness reigned. Somewhere close by a shrill cry sounded, follow-ed by a deep, rumbling roar.

Jack's eyes narrowed and he took a moment to triangulate the direction of the sound. Then he leapt high, soaring high above the walls, willing himself to stop, floating in midair.

He quickly picked up movement, as he spied a small figure below, tearing down the passage at breakneck speed. He willed himself to move, swooping down to a halt just before, what turned out to be, a young boy.

The lad was around five years old, his chubby, little face streaked with grime topped with a thick mop of unkempt black hair. His bare feet were bound in strips of dirty cloth, and his thin legs were naked beneath his flapping tunic. The ancient rags billowed as he ran straight into Jack, then fell back with a piercing scream of absolute terror.

Jack knelt in the snow and offered his hand to the boy. "I wont hurt you," he whispered, his mind in a spin.

The boy began to scrabble backwards, fear, desperation and confusion clouding his round eyes.

"The...the...m...m...monster! Run!"

Jack scooped the wriggling child into his arms and held the sobbing boy tightly, their 'Father-Son' roles reversed. Jack felt an overwhelming urge to protect the child.

"I have come to take the nasty monster away. It will not harm you...Lailoken."

The boy lifted his puffy red face and looked directly into Jack's eyes with a glimmer of hope.

"Promise?"

"Promise," said Jack with a firm nod and a grim smile.

Strangely, Jack's thoughts were clear and concise, as he unconsciously put the fact that Lailoken was his own Father to the back of his mind.

In the months leading up to this point, Jack had discovered the identity of his Father, and also discovered to his dismay, some of the deeds he had committed under the Demon's evil sway.

Jack had a sudden urge to change himself, and with a swift visualisation he became decked in magnificently mirrored armour of shining silversteel plate.

"Remember your schooling, Lailoken. Thought is everything... Knowledge is power!" Jack said tapping the boy three times on the centre of his grimy forehead, setting him down to stand in the snow.

Something changed in the boy's eyes, and a flicker of memory surfaced, reflecting in his face. Moments later he shimmered, his rags transforming into a similar shining armour, in miniature.

"I remembered!" Lailoken beamed with childish glee.

Jack smiled.

A deep growl echoed through the maze, and the lad's confidence vanished. He sprang forward, gripping Jack tightly around one leg.

An undulating, morphing darkness moved towards them, blotting out the light. As huge clawed fists tore chunks out of the solid stone walls, pulling something huge, inexorably towards them.

Lailoken trembled in terror, and began to whimper as Jack steeled himself.

"*Sword*," Jack said quietly, the magnificent weapon instantly appearing, dazzlingly bright in the sunless gloom of the looming black walls.

The Demon stopped and the darkness melted slightly. The huge twisted shape of the monster slowly became apparent. The beast filled the space between the walls, a hulking head with an overfull mouth of sword-sharp teeth, and red-hot eyes of fiery fury, framed on each side by colossal, curled, ram-like horns. Massively bunched muscles knotted across gargantuan shoulders, the rest of the body cloaked in a swirling mist of darkness.

The Demon gave a gurgling laugh and acrid black smoke washed over the snow in a noxious cloud.

"Give me the whelp, Dragonboy. My command of this frame will be complete, and you will suffer as he has."

"He is my Father, Demon." Jack said slowly through gritted teeth. "By the great Lord our Sun," he raised a palm to the sky, "and the mighty earth Goddess." He pointed to the ground, "By the Gods of the forest, the seas and the air." He moved his open palm from right to left before his chest, forming a shining cross of light. "I compel you to exit this body and return to the circle of life."

The Demon gave a hissing, gurgling cry and raised a hand the size of a house. The dark fireball erupted and flew towards Jack and Lailoken.

Jack did not move.

As the fire struck the mirrored suit, it reflected, and by the 'Ancient Law of Three' it reflected threefold. The three balls of fire rebounded back into the face of the dark monstrosity.

Wreathed in flame, the huge Demon shot into the air on midnight wings, arcing into the clouds before sweeping down into some distant part of the maze.

"Wow," cried Lailoken excitedly. "That was fantastic! I thought I was a goner there! When...when I grow up, I'm gonna be a wizard just like you..." Lailoken stopped. He looked around, shaking his head as if dazed. "When...when...I...grow up...I."

Jack knelt in the snow and gripped Lailoken tightly, with a hand on each shoulder. "You have grown up, Lailoken. You are a man..."

Lailoken's small face screwed up into a frown. "What? I...I am..." His faced blurred and suddenly he changed again, sprouting and filling out till he appeared a lanky young man. Tall and slim, with fine features that Jack recognised. Dressed in a simple black, hooded robe.

"Thank you, stranger. My mind has been... elsewhere, whilst the Demon controls my body." Lailoken explained in a soulfully deep voice.

Jack swallowed hard. He reached out and placed a hand on Lailoken's shoulder. "I am Jack. Jack the Changeling."

"Dragonboy?" Lailoken queried with an easy smile, a familiar twinkle in his eye. "I remember the Demon's taunt."

Jack smiled. "Yes, I change into a Dragon. I know you are the Eagle, Lupin is the Wolf and your Father, Belthor is the Bear."

At the mention of Belthor, a pained expression briefly shadowed Lailoken's face. "My Father... he... "

"He loves you, Lailoken. For many years he has searched for you, and even now is in the most dire peril."

Lailoken gave Jack an incredulous look. "How do you know these things, Jack?"

"Belthor is my Grandfather, Lailoken, and you are my Father."

Lailoken's mouth hung open, his eyes round. He frowned, and closed his mouth. "My Son? You...are...my Son?"

Jack nodded, and broke the tension, "I have the Book of Raziel! Come Father, we have a Demon to exorcise."

Lailoken's wide mouth turned up in a wry smile, as he cast a glance at the walls surrounding them. "I don't suppose I need this labyrinth anymore."

The towering walls faded, becoming insubstantial, before dissolving completely, leaving a featureless white wasteland. A dark blot appeared in the distance, filling the white emptiness with towering black clouds.

For a moment, Father and Son stood together, staring at the distant Demon. Jack nodded to himself and took his Father by the hand.

The pair surged across the plain towards the darkness, the snow melting to reveal green grass beneath as they swept along.

The Demon rose to its full height, the cloaking darkness fading. It growled and gnashed mighty teeth, making the two Changelings dive left and right.

"Pathetic." The Demon spat stinking, yellow acid. "Do you really think you can drive me from this puny body?"

Jack shook his head, "No I don't. But you will choose to go fairly soon."

Lailoken gave Jack a strange look, and the monster gave a horrible gurgling laugh.

"You see, I have taken away the gift your Dark Angel gave you. Now you are mortal again, and Lailoken here, is dying. Even now the body is suffocating, desperate for air. In a few moments you and he will be drawn though the Threshold onto the just judgement of the afterlife."

The Demon's cinder eyes narrowed, as Lailoken sank slowly to his knees sobbing. "Forgive me, my son. Please let my Father know that my dying moments were spent thinking of him."

"I have given you one chance, Demon. The chance to leave of your own volition. There is another host nearby, your lackey Riznar's soul is being contained...elsewhere. I will leave this failing body now and use Raziel's book to destroy your Mistress."

The Demon howled and roared with terrible rage, then a twisting cyclone of light surrounded the beast, and with a rumble of thunder it vanished.

"Release him, Gaia." Jack intoned magically; sending a distant thought to Belthor's Sister.

Lailoken looked up at his Son and smiled.

"Breathe," Jack said magically.

Chapter 49

Samanthiel jumped as Riznar's body began to convulse and spasm, rolls of fat shuddering and rippling beneath the loose garment. He jerked and twisted as Riznar and the Demon began the struggle for mastery of the large body. Eventually the two shared the body, and Riznar's eyes snapped open.

He barely managed a gasping intake of breath before Samanthiel leapt, thrusting Nemesis through the soft robe, skewering him through the chest, pinning him to the floor.

"Die, Demon!" She hissed through her clenched teeth, spraying the horrified face with spittle.

*

Jack floated above his body, watching grimly as Samanthiel killed the wizard and Demon in one fell swoop. He waited, witnessing their dying moments; the final thrash of limbs as the body expired.

Then two separate spirits floated slowly free; one vaguely man shaped; the other a formless, pulsating dark mist. Their mental screams of despair and rage echoed through the ether. The dark souls swirled and twisted, urgently trying in vain to re-enter the body.

Suddenly a shimmering doorway formed beside Riznar's body, and a large, brilliantly luminous being stepped through the portal. Jack had to shield himself from the fantastically radiant aura.

The Watcher at the Threshold turned and nodded to Jack, lifting a luminous hand in silent salute.

Then turned and pointed at the Demon.

"I compel you, dark soul, in the name of the Creator and all her Gods. I command you to cross

this, the divine threshold, and face your richly deserved judgement.”

The Demon's dark soul gradually shrank and condensed into a tiny black sphere and shot through the open doorway, on to the afterlife. Then he turned his angelic attention to Riznar's spirit, and he was similarly expelled.

Jack watched enthralled as the holy being carried out his duty and gave a solemn nod before slowly fading along with the doorway.

*

Samanthiel felt the small hairs on the back of her neck rise as Lailoken took a deep breath, staggering forwards from his inanimate state. Slowly the demonic influences faded from his face; the flesh filled out slightly; life returning to his eyes; wasted muscles thickened and grew, as he returned to consciousness.

“Samanthiel, allow me to introduce you to Lailoken, my Father.” Jack said, rising stiffly to his feet.

Lailoken gripped the edge of the damaged seeing table, swaying unsteadily on wobbly legs. He looked down at the healed scarring on his hands, then caught a glimpse of his haggard reflection in the crazed surface of the table. He gave a sharp intake of breath, raising a hand to his cheek slowly.

“How long has the Demon held sway over my body?” He said in a raw whisper.

“Must be fifteen years or more,” Jack said.

“Fifteen years...”

“Belthor searched for you...Lailoken, but Riznar conspired with the Demon and kept your whereabouts well hidden.”

Lailoken turned and scowled at the dead mage.

Samanthiel gave an exasperated grunt, “Enough of the family reunion! Do you forget that Belthor is out there?”

Jack and Lailoken looked at Samanthiel, then at each other. Jack shrugged, raising his eyebrows.

"There is also the small matter of the Fallen Angel to deal with." She added.

"Can you remember anything of the Demon's memories?" Jack asked his Father.

Lailoken shook his head. "Nothing, it's like I've just woken from a long and terrible nightmare."

Jack placed a hand either side of Lailoken's head and closed his eyes, concentrating hard. A faint glow surrounded his fingertips, and slowly the echoes of his possessed memory floated into his mind.

The scene from the deep cavern under the river replayed in his mind's eye; Belthor pinned between the standing stones, half encased in ice and the dark Angel stealing his soul.

Jack gave a low moan and staggered back, dropping his hands.

"She has him." Jack sobbed, large tears forming in his eyes. "His spirit is trapped within a stone spike, Lillith has it... She...she is at the river along with a resurrected army of Demons."

Samanthiel's face twisted into a grimace. "An army of Demons, eh?" She asked. "We'll have to get his soul back then." She added with simple logic.

Jack pulled himself together. "The Demon ordered the destruction of the forests, and half the gathered army is off doing just that. Father, you can stop them. They still think of you as Lord Lailoken ...change their hearts..."

Lailoken nodded. "I think I understand what you are asking for, Jack."

He moved to the open window, unfastening his robes. Before changing, he turned. "Jack, Samanthiel, thank you for saving me."

He did not wait for a reply, but stepped out onto the balcony and out of sight.

Jack turned to Samanthiel.

"Want to kill some more Demons, Sam?"

She raised her top lip in a snarl. "Does a Dragon breath fire?" Her snarling lips twisting into a fierce smile.

"You are gonna love this! Teeth, claws and fire, what more could a girl ask for?" Jack laughed.

Chapter 50

Alvor, the Protectors and several mages gathered in the deep shadows at the edge of a forest clearing. The young apprentice, Jared, hunkered down among the bushes, beside the silent men.

He had known that there had been a large group of men following them through the forest, but using a few basic concealment spells he had hidden their trail well. Using cunning, stealth and a great deal of luck he'd led the column of civilians safely through the forest, successfully meeting up with the Master Alvor and the rest of the Darkhaven refugees.

Then the message from Lord Ness came through. The masters and the elders quickly decided to act against the dark Angel, Lillith. Gathering every able bodied and willing man and woman, they left a small contingent of troops to protect the elderly and young, before turning to face their pursuers.

Now Jared sat quietly in the frontline, concentrating deeply on keeping a mental shield intact. Ahead in the clearing camped hundreds of troops and a group of mages; their colourful tents in the centre surrounded by sentries. They believed that their quarry was still fleeing and were arrogant in their confidence; not one sentry stood at the forest's edge.

Alvor motioned to the other wizards, and they spread in a wide semicircle around the large glade. They planned to send out a magical concussive wave of confusion before the Protectors and the volunteer troops stormed the camp.

He closed his eyes, trying to create a mental whirlwind of chaos. The feeling of turbulent power grew within him. The surrounding line of masters followed suit.

A screech broke the silence. The silhouette of an eagle swept past the sun, glided gracefully into the camp. Moments later a soft flash of light pulsed between the tents, and cries of alarm filled the air.

Alvor cursed as his concentration was broken, the confusion spell dissipating harmlessly. Then a pulse of energy swept outwards from the centre of camp, not the dark magic he expected but the cleansing earth power of the Goddess Danu.

Around him the other mages muttered in confusion, and began to rise from their hidden positions. Jared looked up at his old master, thrown by the unexpected sensation. Alvor's wrinkled face broke into a wide smile as the camped troops began dropping weapons and falling to their knees, weeping loudly. He stepped from the shadows, followed warily by Jared and the remainder of the Darkhaven magic council.

Lailoken appeared from between the tents, wrapping a dark robe around his slim frame. He smiled as he clapped eyes on Alvor and the others approaching.

"Greetings, Master Alvor. Thank the Goddess! You have saved us a great deal of time!" Lailoken cried with relief.

As Alvor entered the glade, he began to chuckle, "Young Lailoken, so you have decided to come home. Your father will be happy, lad."

A small frown crossed Lailoken's face. "Have you not heard? Belthor has been taken. Lillith holds his soul in a necromius spine!"

The smile and the colour fled from Alvor's face, the foul news staggering him.

"I knew he was captive... but... but I never thought he would... fall." He sniffed loudly, wiping a sleeve across his eyes.

"All is not lost, Master. Jack the Changeling has acquired Raiziel's book. We must make haste back to the river and help him face this dark threat, and hopefully rescue my Father's soul!"

Alvor looked on as the people of Darkhaven mustered around them, the converted troops and the Protectors uniting as one army.

"Men of Darkhaven, you have heard Lailoken's words. Recently we have all suffered under the dark shadow of evil, but now the time of testing is upon us. The light is returning, fighting back in the shape of a Dragon. Yes, my friends, a Dragon. We must become warriors of that light and march to aid this Dragon, to help him to banish the darkness for ever!"

As one the people of Darkhaven began to cheer. Jared roared his approval at Alvor's stirring speech, excitement flooding through his young body.

Chapter 51

Lupin bounded through the long grass, his large paws flying and long tongue lolling as he panted. The long hilly ridge, that ran north into the foothills of the Giant's Teeth Mountains, sloped gently eastwards down to the wide river Ulfen below. As he crested the ridge he came to a skidding stop. He caught his breath and gave a long, high-pitched howl; signalling to the distant scouts behind in the hills.

*

Lord Ness pulled on the reins and Thunder came to a halt beside the large black wolf. The view of the river below took away his breath; the churning water was covered with a creeping crusty sheet of ice approaching the near shore.

Captain Reed cantered up the hill behind them and swearing softly as the scene below tore at his attention.

"Sir, the infantry is... several hours behind and the... horses are going to arrive soon." Reed informed, continually glancing down at the creeping white bridge.

Ness removed his helmet, setting it on the saddle pommel before dismounting. He placed a gauntleted hand on Lupin's high shoulder. "What have we got to do to stop these creatures, lad?" Ness sighed wearily.

Lupin sat on his haunches, looking up with bright eyes, communicating mentally. "My Brothers and Sisters are in the foothills to the north. We will mass on this ridge by the light of the full moon tonight."

Ness smiled and shook his head, "No, Lupin. I want you to take your wolf-kin westwards to safety. They sacrificed much in the last battle, and it will take several seasons for the packs to replenish."

Lupin interrupted with a soft growl and bared teeth, "My father is across there with those monsters, Lord Ness. I will not abandon him. Nor do I think that my Brothers and Sisters will sit idly by and watch the scourge, they fought so hard to help defeat, cross this river and destroy these lands."

Ness's bushy brow raised, and he gave a small chuckle of resignation. "I had to try, lad. I had to try."

He turned to Captain Reed. "Come, Reed. We need to talk strategy."

*

Samanthiel rose, resplendent in her Dragon form, jet scales reflecting the sun in their smoky depths. She shook her head dismissing the pain, stretching her dark wings. The unseeing eyes of the plaza statues bore silent witness to her change, as Jack roared his joy and swooped from the sky in a great gust of back-flaps of his huge green wings, before alighting gently on the deserted platform.

"Sam, you look fantastic!" Jack cried, gnashing his teeth in admiration of her new form.

She gripped her small leather pack and scabbard in one clawed foot and gave a tentative flap of her wings, ignoring the compliment. Her forelegs rose slightly. She tensed her new muscles, beating the leathery wing steadily harder and faster.

"Take a deep breath. It helps to make you lighter." Jack advised.

Slowly Samanthiel rose into the air, hovering with a steady beat of her wings.

"Lock your shoulder joints! Straighten your wingtips and glide...it's easy!" Jack shouted from the ground, beginning to flap his own wings.

Samanthiel turned her attention to the horizon, and followed Jack's instruction. She soared forwards, gliding over the plaza edge high over the empty city. Tilting one way, then the other, she banked left and right curving gracefully before rising again on a powerful gusty flap.

Samanthiel began to laugh. A delighted glee flooded through her long serpentine form.

I'm flying! She cried to herself, *I'm really flying!* Roaring into the afternoon sky, Samanthiel swooped and banked; her confidence growing with every beat of her huge heart.

A trembling sensation of excitement grew within her stomachs, acids mixed and gasses boiled deep within her. She tightened her muscles and exhaled a roiling roar of flames.

"Yes!" Jack roared. "You are ready!"

Moments later Jack joined her wingtip and together they wheeled westwards towards the shining ribbon of the river.

Chapter 52

Belthor's soul twisted helplessly in a dark vortex of cosmic wind, as Lillith diverted the massive potential energy of the river into the growing plate of ice.

He could only observe as she perched like a dark gargoyle on the tip of an iceberg, crouching with arms outstretched and head low in concentration.

She could feel the presence of the humans on the near shore; massing on the ridge. She was darkly delighted that her new children would not have to wait long to feed.

"Can you feel them, Belthor? Your family and friends are waiting to die!" Lillith's spirit spat at him, though her head was bowed in concentration.

"The Creator and her Gods will not give you a free hand to destroy mankind, Lillith. Soon you will face their judgement." Belthor said calmly.

The swirling black of her midnight aura flashed red with anger, before settling to darkness once again. Belthor sought to distract her, attempting to stop the completion of the bridge.

"I will destroy the Gods, and all life with the secrets of my learned Brother, Raziel. The fool gathered all the knowledge I will need, and at this moment my servant is bringing the book to me."

"Time will tell," Belthor said, watching as the near shore drew inexorably closer.

*

A frown marred Lillith's perfect face, as she cast her gaze back over the river.

Where is he? She thought impatiently. Belthor's chuckle further enraged her and she sent a ball of astral fire at the imprisoned soul.

As the sun set and full moon rose above the ridge, the ice kissed the western shore, rapidly thickening and creeping half way up the ridge; turning the scene wintry.

At Lillith's signal, the newborn Demon horde swept onto the ice bridge, leaving the far shore littered with the burnt out husks of half the Darkhaven army.

*

Samanthiel and Jack roared in unison, swooping from a twilight sky, claws extended. On the ice the skittering Demons cried their defiance. Jack's mind expanded as his thoughts and new knowledge jostled for attention. A single spell leapt unbidden from behind the dark curtain of his subconscious, then flew from his throat.

"Cleanse." Jack's voice spread a magical pulse of power from deep within himself, destroying the dark, possessing magic of the monsters on the ice.

Instantly a distant shriek of rage pierced the night as Lillith took to the wing, shooting into the darkening sky like a black falcon.

*

Samanthiel swooped across the frozen bridge, tearing several creatures with her razor talons, roaring in jubilation, before dropping them into the swirling foam. She banked in a tight turn, taking a deep breath; before transforming several more Demons into burning beacons. The Demons raced across the ice, claws giving good grip on the glassy surface.

Samanthiel gave an ear shattering roar, as Jack copied her tactics. He swept past her wing in the opposite direction, a flaming rain roasting dozens in his wake.

*

At the unexpected arrival of the Dragons, Lord Ness, Sigurd and the foot soldiers poured down the slope on foot, charging headlong across the ice to meet the oncoming monsters.

*

Lillith screamed into the sky, eyes wide with disbelief: her precious offspring were now being cut down in droves. Rage twisted her divine innards as she hung in the air above the battle line. Summoning a ball of dark power, she loosed it onto the battling creatures below.

Instantly the fallen, both Demon and mankind, began to convulse and twitch with unnatural life.

*

Lord Ness and Sigurd fought in the front line. Ness's sword expertly dispatched Demons with careful precision, whilst a berserk Sigurd waded forwards, roaring mindlessly, his huge stone axe a bloody, black whirlwind.

These Demons were larger and stronger than the portal-crossing Demons he had faced outside the gates of his city, but Lord Ness fought heroically; till a spear point took him between the shoulder blades, piercing his armour.

He gave a short cry, twisting around to see the bloody, vacant stare of his attacker; the soldier was dead; a ragged wound torn across his face and neck, yet now the undead soldier stood ready to kill his comrades.

A blurred shadow removed the man's head, the great stone axe sending it rolling into the swirling water, leaving the body to collapse onto the crimson ice.

Sigurd hefted Lord Ness upon one strong shoulder and began fighting his way through the shambling ranks of the undead, towards the shore.

*

Satisfied that the Demons were gaining the upper hand against the humans, Lillith turned her attention to the pair of Dragons harrying her offspring.

She shot through the air, gathering speed before delivering a stunning blow; striking Samanthiel with a magical stone fist. Samanthiel gave a winded screech of pain as several of her ribs splintered and broke. She plummeted towards the boiling foam, wings flapping ineffectually.

Jack folded his own wings, falling into a hawk-like dive, opening them and racing low over the ice, before rising to support his falling friend.

Lillith sneered and was about to strike again, when an arrow zipped past, close to her face, rapidly followed by several more. She peeled off, swooping down to the relative safety of the craggy ice.

*

Alvor, Lailoken and the people of Darkhaven stormed down the riverbank onto the ice, the mental shield that had hidden their arrival, no longer necessary.

Archers loosed volley after volley at the dark figure on the ice, though every arrow was easily deflected by her immense powers. The mages gathered power, ready to deflect any magic the dark Angel summoned.

*

Sigurd, Ness and the foot soldiers fell back, fighting an orderly retreat back up the ridge. The Demons rushed to follow, the undead staggering steadily behind them.

As the footmen formed ranks, and the Demons swept off the ice onto the slope, Sigurd blew a long high note on his horn.

The thunder of hooves shook the ground, as two units of cavalry moved into a flanking attack, lances and spears levelled, riding hard in arrowhead formations.

A reserve of burly Grimswadian troops pushed through the beleaguered line of defenders, hurtling down the slope in a melee attack, slamming into the confused enemy.

At Lupin's howl the wolves followed close behind the horses, tearing and snapping at the undead in a furious series of skirmishing attacks.

*

The peppering of arrows ceased as the obvious futility of the attack became apparent. Fire blazed in Lillith's dark eyes. She slowly approached Alvor and the Darkhaven folk; each step sending the ice steaming with her hot footsteps. She was determined to see each and every one of these humans burn to cinders.

Chapter 53

A fierce battle raged on the western shore, and to the east Lillith approached the people of Darkhaven, as Jack guided Samanthiel safely to the ice. She collapsed, lowering her head, panting in breathless agony.

He was horrified at the broken dent in her plate scales, and knew that she must be suffering greatly.

"Go and...save...Belthor..." Samanthiel gasped, dark blood dripping from her snout, staining the ice.

Jack's lips peeled back as he roared loudly, sending a jet of flame into the night. He took a deep breath and launched himself skywards.

Knowledge is power, he thought, feeling for something within.

He swept low across the ice, his wingtips barely clearing the water. In moments he shot over Lillith, skidding to a stop between her and the citizens of Darkhaven.

"Stop!" Jack cried, but the immobilisation spell had no effect on the Angel.

Lillith's eyes narrowed and then she gave a sneering laugh. "You have Raziel's book within you and you do not know how to use it properly! I shall tear the knowledge from your tortured soul," she declared.

"Enough!" Jack roared furiously, stomping forwards quickly, raising a huge clawed foot, and sending a fireball rolling across the ice. The flames smoothed the ice into a shining path, but split harmlessly either side of Lillith's outstretched arms.

Jack was about to flatten the Angel, when she moved impossibly quickly from beneath his foot. She whipped the glistening stone spike from her armour and thrust it into

Jack's chest plate, the point piercing his scales with magical ease.

Across the ice Samanthiel screamed.

Jack whipped his serpentine neck skywards and roared in agony. Below him Lillith laughed, twisting and pushing the spike deeper still, till the point almost reached his heart.

Suddenly Jack stopped roaring and looked down at the Angel with a hard, determined gaze.

"Break."

Lillith gave a sharp gasp as the stone in her hand twisted and expelled itself from the chest plate, then shattered into fragments.

With a stunning swipe, Jack sent Lillith sprawling off the bridge, upstream into the bubbling foam. She disappeared beneath the waves without a sound.

Jack sensed the soul of his Grandfather spiralling off back to his body, with a mental warning echoing into his head, "Beware...Jack...beware..."

Suddenly a black shape erupted from the river, shooting skywards in a deadly arc, before swooping arrow-fast to strike Jack. He moved swiftly with the magic of the Gods and countered Lillith's deadly attack with a lash of his barbed tail, swatting the dark angel from the air. She smashed heavily into the ice, sending a spider-web fracture running through the frozen bridge. Jack followed up with a jet of rage-fuelled flame.

A curtain of steam and lingering fog surrounded the fallen Angel, as Jack approached ready to finish the battle. She rose to a kneeling position as Jack loomed over her ready snap her up in his massive mouth. Her dark, stone gauntlet shot up and she took hold of Jack's chin.

Instantly a wreath of black fire encircled Jack's head, charring his scales. A red-hot ring of agony seared his neck and he screamed rearing up. Lillith held fast, dangling from his jaw chanting the fire spell.

"Jack!" Samanthiel's cry filtered through the pain.

*

Lailoken and Alvor rushed onto the ice as Jack furiously tried to dislodge Lillith; desperately whipping her back and forth. Alvor gripped Lailoken's arm, shouting over Jack's pained scream. "Lailoken! We must summon Nemmius!"

Lailoken's eyes narrowed and he cast an urgent glance at his son. He shook his head, "You do it, Alvor. I must try and save Jack!"

Alvor nodded and Lailoken ran on, leaving the old man to gather his energy and sink to his knees in preparation.

"The water, Jack. It is your only hope." Lailoken shouted at the frantic Dragon.

Taking his Father's advice, Jack leapt from the bridge and plunged into the freezing tumble of turbulent water. Instantly the dark flames quelled and relief flooded through him. The current swept him downriver away from the bridge of ice, dragging him into the murky depths. He was dimly aware of the fist still clinging to his chin.

He began kicking and flapping in the water, making little headway; memories of the swim through the dark tunnels of Grimswade floated into his mind and panic flooded though him.

Suddenly a deep, booming voice entered his head. **"A Dragon in my depths?"**

Through the watery gloom a bubbling glow approached. Large pockets of silvery air formed beneath Jack's wings, lending buoyancy and rushing him upwards.

Jack broke the surface and Lillith let go of his jaw and shot skywards, circling back in a sweeping arc to land on the bridge. He took a deep breath, and with several flaps and a tremendous effort broke free of the sucking eddies.

As he rose into the air the swirling waters beneath began to churn, the white foam transforming as several beasts began to rise from the depths. A huge stone and seaweed chariot rose, pulled by massive horses made from a mixture of water and sand, the swirling white foam forming their manes, and long tangles of kelp their tails.

Standing alone on the footplate was Nemmius - God of the sea - a huge being of shells and sea-smoothed stone, holding a massive barnacle covered trident in one giant-clam fist and the ropey tangles of seaweed reins in the other.

He turned towards the angel, fixing her with a watery gaze, deep as the seabed, his voice the deep rumble of an ocean storm.

"Lillith the Fallen. I thought we imprisoned you many aeons ago... Come forth Brothers and Sisters!"

He hefted the trident, light lancing skywards from the encrusted tines. Mighty winds blew from every direction, smoke-like clouds gathering and condensing into towering thunderheads. Each gust swirled and swept them together into a looming lightning-lit figure of Ariel - Goddess of the Storm.

She raised her thunderous arms and pointed wispy fingers at the western shore. The earth began to shake and split, the quake sending the battling armies to their knees. Bolts of lightning shot into the hillside, the earth swelling and braking as Danu rose into her rock and fire form, straddling the ridge with a volcanic glow.

She raised a rocky fist and threw a ball of molten stone in a high arc, landing with a bright splash of crimson fire on the opposite bank. The orange flames faded, instantly replaced by the luminous, green glow of Lord Cerranos, striding purposefully down the bare hillside towards the people of Darkhaven.

Lillith tried to escape into the sky, but Jack swooped.

"Freeze!"

As the true magic of the Gods encircled her, she did just that and froze in midair, suspended by the power of the spell. Jack swept past the immobile Angel, out over the Demons and undead soldiers.

"Cleanse!"

The undead slumped and fell to their final rest, while the Demons gave one last howl of desperation, before crumbling into glowing embers.

Jack glided down to settle on the ice beside Samanthiel and turned to face the Angel.

Chapter 54

Nemmius looked down at Lillith and slowly shook his watery head.

"I do not understand your motivation, Angel Lillith. You were the brightest and best of the heavenly host, but now the darkness within you has shadowed your soul deeper than any watery abyss."

He looked to his divine Brother and Sisters in turn, communing silently before giving a solemn nod. Raising his trident, he gave a gurgling command.

Impossibly the raging river water stopped flowing, turning flat and mirror smooth. Slowly a silvery ball of water rose into the night sky, emulating the full-moon. Lillith could only observe as the sphere moved through the air, enveloping her in the cold ball of water.

In the sky Ariel's cumulus chest expanded as she drew in an expansive breath, before bending and blowing with an intensely cold wind. The sphere crackled and froze solid in her bitter breath.

Danu raised her arm and spread molten fingers; weaving a lattice of glowing rock. She blew with a volcanic breath, and the net of stone wafted through the air and wrapped around the icy ball, where Ariel's breath solidified it instantly.

Cerranos closed his glowing green eyes, reaching out with one leafy hand, pointing down at the rich, torn earth at his rooted feet.

"Grow!" He whispered with the sound of the wind through leafy branches.

A row of mighty trees sprang into life, growing strong and tall. The trees rose on lengthy roots, moving to the riverbank before toppling into the water, sending waves rippling across the lake-like surface. Vines and creepers sprouted and grew, snaking between the trunks; tightening and pulling the trees into a massive raft.

Nemmius gestured with his trident and the raft moved to sit beneath the hovering ball of ice and rock. He gave another small movement and the sphere lowered to settle on the raft; the wood groaning and creaking under the immense weight. Several more roots and vines wove into thick rope and secured the ball in place.

Nemmius swept his gaze east and west.

"We have all given freely of ourselves. Now you humans must give... A sacrifice is required to bind the dark Angel."

He paused, before asking: **"Who will offer their lifeblood to seal the binding?"**

*

Jack rose wearily to his feet. "I will. Take me."

Nemmius gave a nod and was about to speak when Samanthiel cut him off.

"No! I am injured, take me in his place," she cried anxiously. Suddenly she gasped in surprise and pain as a surge of energy flowed through the ice.

Jack finished with a single word.

"Heal."

She whipped her dark head round, anger flashing in her slitted eyes.

"Jack...No!"

A howling cry sounded off to the west as a dark wolf sped towards them, followed closely by the Lord Ness and Sigurd hurrying as best they could across the ice.

Another shout of anguish sounded as Lailoken ran from the east shouting. "No...Jack!"

Jack took a deep breath, blocking out the cries, resigning himself to the sacrifice, as a solitary tear ran down his nose, dripping from his snout. Two flaps of his wings lifted him clear of the bridge and he glided towards the raft.

Samanthiel reared up and roared, issuing a bright flame towards the stars. She began to flap her wings desperately, but in her grief and panic forgot to inhale fully, and merely floundered on the ice.

"Jack!" Samanthiel cried, "Please don't leave... me."

*

Jack gave a roar of his own, apprehension twisting his innards as he remembered Ulfner Darkbane's skeletal form pinned to the table within the Dragon's eyrie. Yet onwards he flew, circling the raft as Sigurd, Ness and Lailoken met with Samanthiel.

As Jack alighted gently upon the icy ball, a surge of energy rushed up through his feet. Jack could feel Lillith's hatred seething and boiling; the sheer power of her rage left him breathless and dizzy.

Suddenly a peal of thunder shattered the night and Jack was astonished when a dark shape swooped from the clouds, passing between the towering Goddess Ariel's legs.

A Dragon? Jack thought in detached amazement, then he recognised the little woman riding the dark-green beast, her long silver hair flowing in the wind. *Gaia?*

His stomach lurched and a sickening dread swept through him when he saw that the Dragon cradled Belthor gently within a careful claw.

The green Dragon landed on the raft beside the ball, placing Belthor upon a bed of leaves. Gaia leapt nimbly to his side, her complexion ashen.

*

On the bridge Lailoken cried out magically, and in a changeling flash he transformed into his eagle shape, gripping his cloak in sharp talons. Lupin howled his sorrow to his lunar Sister and changed back to human form. Ness unclipped his cloak, wrapping it around the shivering man.

"Samanthiel...can you carry me?" Lupin looked deep into her eyes, and she blinked away a freezing tear.

Lord Ness quickly unbuckled his sword and removed the belt, wrapping the thick leather around one wrist before offering the other end to Sigurd. He frowned and took hold.

Seeing what Ness intended, Samanthiel took hold of the middle of the belt and lifted the pair easily into the air. Then she gripped Lupin carefully around his waist.

Taking a very deep breath, she felt her weight lighten as the gasses inside her changed. Then two flaps later she glided to the others on the raft.

The Gods bore silent witness as the family of Changelings and their friends began reuniting on the raft.

*

Belthor coughed as Gaia applied a leaf to his raw chest wound. His naked body was burned with fire and ice. Each beat of his heart sent waves of agony through his ravaged frame.

"Please...Sister, stop." Belthor gasped raggedly.

Jack leapt from the ball, watching as Lailoken changed himself back into human form, lifting his robe back over his shoulders.

Jack lowered his snout, warming his Grandfather with his hot breath.

"I will heal you, Belthor. I know how..."

"Jack...you did it. You...retrieved Raziel's book, and you have freed...your Father. I knew...you were the Chosen...one."

Belthor wheezed, coughing as bright blood flecked his pale lips, before continuing. "Your work is done, Jack...Now you ...and Samanthiel must continue...the Changeling line."

Fresh tears began to drip from Jack's snout as Lailoken approached, quickly kneeling and placing a kiss on Belthor's blackened forehead, whispering, "Father... Please forgive me..."

"Lailoken,...my son..." Tears welled in Belthor's sunken eyes, "...there is... nothing... to forgive. I should... have seen the signs... please forgive me, Lailoken."

Lailoken wept silently as Belthor gripped his hand hard, even though the skin was blistered and scorched.

"Lupin...is he...?"

"I am here, Father!" Lupin sobbed, kneeling at his other side, tears running freely down his face.

Belthor raised his other burned hand and placed it on his Son's shoulder, "Look after...Jack and Samanthiel, Lupin... they are important..."

Lupin nodded, looking up at the watching Dragons. "I will, Father."

Lupin looked at his long lost Brother for a moment, and smiled through his tears, before kissing Belthor on both cheeks.

"Goodbye Father, we will run together between the stars one day!"

Each beat of Jack's Dragon heart pulsed painfully within his throat as he longed to hug the old man; but he had a prophecy to fulfil.

As he was about to climb back onto the sphere, Belthor called out in a surprisingly clear and powerful voice.

"Nemmius, God of the Water; Danu, Goddess of the Earth; Cerrenos, God of Life; Ariel, Goddess of the Air, bear witness! I, Belthor, will sacrifice what little life I still possess to create a new binding here this night!"

Jack's snout whipped around in panic and he gave a loud roar of fright, more icy tears dripping from his chin. "No!"

Nemmius lifted his trident, and slowly Belthor floated through the air, landing gently in an upright position with his burned back to the cold, curved surface of the ball.

"Belthor, your sacrifice will be remembered for all eternity... Step forwards and commence the binding!"

Gaia stood and reached up, snapping off a long icicle of Dragon tears hanging from Jack's jaw. She proceeded to hold the icy spike skywards, intoning in a power filled voice -

"ATEH!"

Then she passed the ice to Lailoken, who nodded sadly before crying -

"MALKUTH!"

He passed the spike to Lupin, who did not hesitate -

"VE GEBBURAH!"

The ice began to glow with an inner light, pulsing with the colours of the rainbow, Lupin passed the shard to Ness who shouted -

"VE GEDDULAH!"

He passed the spike to Sigurd, who, though he knew no magic, was compelled to cry out in a deep, booming voice -

"LA OHLAM!"

As one the four deities above intoned -

"AMEN!"

Sigurd passed the bright ice back to Gaia and she lifted the leaf from Belthor's chest, whispering, "I will join you soon, dear Brother."

As Gaia plunged the magical spike into Belthor's wound-ed chest, Lailoken gave a terrible cry of sorrow and loss.

Belthor's threw his head back and cried out in agony, vibrating for a moment before glowing with an incandescent internal light. Swirling symbols began to shine through his almost transparent skin, and as his lifeblood stained the stone and ice, the fiery runes of the mighty bind etched themselves magically into the rock.

In a flash of brilliance Belthor's earthly remains melted into the stone and vanished, his soul journeying onwards through the threshold to the afterlife.

Continuous lightning flashed in a bright vortex, swirling down from the heavens above, turning night to day. The elemental energy lanced into the sphere stabbing repeatedly on all sides till the rock strands melted together into a flawless glassy surface, and the air hung heavy with the pungent aroma of ozone.

Jack raised his head skywards and roared to the Gods, a riot of grief and guilt twisting him inside out.

Suddenly a gargantuan peal of thunder crashed as the Goddess Ariel pointed at the heavens, the chaotic sky splitting open to reveal a single shooting star streaking across the darkness of the void. The light stopped still in the swirling sky, brightening and growing, forming a familiar shape.

Jack gave a gasp of recognition as an Angel floated gracefully down to hover above the glassy prison.

"Raziel!" He cried.

Raziel folded his beautiful wings behind his radiant, silver chainmail armour, removing his Dragon helmet. His noble brow furrowed in sorrow as the malevolence of his dark Sister filtered through the binding and bright tears formed in his eyes. He looked down at Jack and the gathered friends.

"Young Master Jack, you have something that I think might be best kept...elsewhere..."

He reached inside his shimmering sleeve and produced a small book, and slowly glided forwards to place a cool hand against Jack's bony brow.

Jack felt a powerful surge of knowledge and memory, flowing from him, through Raziel's hand into the new book.

He was left with a strange fuzzy feeling as Raziel's voice entered his mind.

"You have many unanswered questions, Jack. I will answer one only, before taking this sphere south to the hostile ice-wastes where no human being can survive; Lillith's frozen prison for the rest of eternity."

Jack cast his gaze left and right; it seemed that his friends did not hear the Angel's words. Thoughts and questions sparred for attention as he considered Raziel's words.

I want to know of my Mother, Jack thought to the Angel.

A sad smile crossed the Angel's face.

"Look to the east. Seek the Tiger's eye, Jack." Raziel said cryptically, before unfolding his glorious wings, tucking the small book back into the folds of his sleeve.

Then with an angelic word of power, Raziel moved everyone from the raft back onto the icebridge, before settling beside the sphere alone. The sea God, Nemmius gave a sweeping gesture with his trident and the waters of the Ulfen sprang back into life, sweeping the raft swiftly downriver and out of sight.

*

One by one the Gods nodded their approval, before Danu spoke.

"Once again, young Jack. You, your family and your companions have served us well. What gift would you ask in return for your service?"

Jack was thrown by the question, still in turmoil over the loss of his Grandfather. Samanthiel nestled closer to him, her presence comforting.

He considered the question before answering.

"This land, and the people have been shattered by an evil deception, and divided by this mighty river. My one request of the Gods is to raise and restore the river city of Ulfenspan!"

Epilogue

Lord Ness rode Thunder along the dusty road leading to his city. All around him the green shoots of new life pushed through the scorched earth as nature returned to his blighted lands. The nutrient rich earth would feed his people once again. He heaved a sigh, a deep sense of relief filling his tired frame. He leant forwards and reached back, rubbing feeling back into his saddle sore behind.

We really need to get out more, old friend! Thunder whinnied and Ness gave him a loving pat.

Approaching the gates he stopped, watching as a young girl rode by in thick padded training armour. She struggled determinedly to level a heavy wooden practice lance; the padded tip weighted to help the recruits build upper body strength.

She rode Star, the chestnut steed, guiding him with her thighs, whilst holding a cumbersome wooden shield. The young knights training nearby stopped and watched as she rode into the fenced-off practice ground. The tip of the lance wavered and bobbed this way and that, as she encouraged her horse, sending him into a swift gallop. Star thundered along as she bore down on her intended straw filled victim.

Ness smiled as she managed to strike the dummy, holding a small circular target shield, sending it spinning as she galloped past giving a savage whoop of joy.

She tipped the lance skywards in a happy salute to her unexpected audience. Ness nodded before continuing homewards.

*

A small blonde lad ran through the streets of Darkhaven. He wound his way through the maze heading through the poor quarter of the capital. He stopped outside his home, his small heart racing.

Suddenly he became aware of a sparkling shape in the gloom of the alleyway.

Belthor's spirit watched, nodding in satisfaction as the door opened and a woman's cry of joy filled the street, and the lad was swept up in a tearful embrace.

*

Lailoken and Alvor stood on the high plaza, watching as Jared oversaw the cleaning of the square; sending groups of apprentices out with scrubbing brushes and mops, scouring the marble till it shone.

Jared had proven himself a worthy leader of men and the remaining councillors had voted overwhelmingly to appoint him the youth leader.

Alvor had returned to the plaza and rescued the wandering souls, as Belthor had promised; opening the portal and guiding them on to the afterlife. Now he shouted unwanted help at the flame-haired lad. "Over there, Jared. Clean that statue!" He pointed with his staff and the lad heaved a sigh, grabbing a bucket of soapy water.

Lailoken laughed and took up a broom, sweeping with the youngsters.

Alvor scowled and turned to inspect the work of the craftsman chipping away at the newest statue, working on the roughly hewn plinth, engraving scrolling letters. The man stopped working, looking up at the old mage with a worried look on his face.

A lump rose in Alvor's throat as he looked up at the larger than life image of his old friend Belthor, surrounded by an even larger stone representation of a great bear, the effect was stunning and he nodded, giving his rare seal of approval.

*

Sigurd and an entourage of Grimswadian tradesman sat respectfully on the hard packed earthen floor of Gaia's hut.

"Old Mother, I have come to right the wrongs against you and your...children." Sigurd spoke slowly and in an over-loud voice.

"I'm old, Lord Grim. Not deaf..." Gaia laughed.

Sigurd apologised and lowered his voice. "I have brought the finest craftsmen from my city. I intend to help you with the clearing of this dank forest and the rebuilding and restor-ation of the temple of the Gods!"

"That is a noble gesture, Sigurd, but I think that Danu and Cerranos might have something to say if you began to harm their trees." Gaia said in a semi-serious tone.

Sigurd paled.

"The temple is fine as it is." She paused, thinking, before continuing, "I think you can do something though."

Sigurd sat straighter, listening.

"Several of my children have chosen human form, and I think it would benefit them if you would accept them into your city, teach them and in return..."

Gaia gave two small claps of her hands, and the doorway in the back of the hut opened and two green skinned men pulled a massive chest into the room. They struggled, lifting the heavy lid, revealing a horde of jewels, gold and silver.

She waited a moment, before adding, "...this will be yours."

The Grimswadians all gasped at the same time.

*

Samanthiel stood on the riverbank staring upwards. The city of Ulfenspan stood again, the same, yet different; every-thing was new, shining and clean. She found it a bit unsettling and struggled to hold her emotions in check, brushing away an annoying tear as painful memories made butterflies flutter in her tightening stomach.

The people who had began to settle in makeshift townships along the eastern shores were still warily returning to their homes. A warm hand took hers and she turned to Jack, who stood silently at her side staring up at the towering building, he gave her cold hand a reassuring squeeze as together they climbed the massive drawbridge ramp and entered the tower.

As they entered the upper hall, her grip on Jack's hand tightened. He glanced at her and she swallowed hard.

They climbed several flights of stairs and out onto the bridge street, stopping at the Keystone Inn. A tiny songbird sang on the swinging sign.

They pushed open the door and a wave of delicious aroma wafted to greet them. A serving maid showed them to a bay window overlooking the rushing water below and the distant clouded shadows of the Giant's Teeth mountains. A thin, white line crossed the river a few miles to the north; Lillith's ice bridge had not melted.

"What are we going to do now, Jack?" Samanthiel asked, as they tucked in to a hearty meal.

Jack did not reply. He sat with a chunk of beef on the tip of his fork, staring at the distant bridge.

"Jack?"

He shook himself from his thoughts. "Eh? Sorry, Sam, I was miles away."

She sighed with pretended exasperation, "I *said*, what now, Dragonboy?"

Jack thought back to the Angel Raziel's words.

Jack spoke in a whisper. "East, Sam. I think... I will go to Darkhaven and onwards...I am going to look for my ...Mother."

Samanthiel frowned. "You mean we. We will go and search for your Mother."

Jack jammed the fork into his mouth and chomped noisily. "Eat up then, Sam. We have a long flight ahead."

The End...

Look out for Book3 in the future!

Coming Soon

Gaia's Sword- A Dragon's Revenge

Snowthorn was a dragon filled with a terrible rage.

They abducted his Father!

They murdered his Mother!

They tore his family apart!

They were the Annunaki - terrible beings from the distant planet Nibru, seemingly bent on raping the Mother Earth of her natural resources...

Desperate for gold!

But Snowthorn was going to stop them.

Helped on his virtuous quest for revenge by his Brother and Sister. He was trained by the Old Blind Oracle and magically empowered by the Earth Goddess Gaia, becoming her champion, her Sword.

Omens are sought and found, and Ancient Prophecies are fulfilled. The boundary of death is crossed and conquered.

Gaia's Sword is an epic retelling of the creation mythology on a grand scale. As seen from the point of view of a Snow Dragon – Snowthorn. Based loosely around the ancient Mesopotamian Legends of the Annunaki.

Dear reader,

Thank you for buying this book! I sincerely hope you enjoyed reading this, as much as I have enjoyed writing it!

Please visit my printer's webpages and leave ANY sort of comments!?

www.lulu.com/ changelings

Click on the book and leave a comment…

'Gaia's Sword' is edited and is going to be illustrated by an up and coming Bolivian Artist called Christian

Eventually there *will* be a Changelings book 3, tentatively entitled ~ "The Tiger's eye" please be patient…

Check out my forthcoming website – www. Jamesmcvean. co. uk

James A. McVean   14/09/06